"Laney," Max said, putting his hands on her shoulders.

Her breathing hitched. When God made those eyes, she thought, he must have mixed in just a little bit of the sky, the windswept California sky where the ocean met the air. She readied herself for a directive. Instead, he offered a request.

"Do something for me." He leaned close. "Please do not leave this training facility for any reason unless I'm with you."

"I'm not a prisoner here, am I?"

"Not a prisoner, but much too important to risk anything happening." He put a finger to her lips when she started to respond. "Not because of the skating, Laney."

"Why, then?" she whispered.

"Because..." He blew out a breath. "Just do what I'm asking. Will you?"

Why did his fingers awaken trails of longing in her soul?

"I'm not going to lie to you, Max," she breathed.

"And I appreciate that."

"So I'm not going to answer at all."

Books by Dana Mentink

Love Inspired Suspense

DANA MENTINK

lives in California, where the weather is golden and the cheese divine. Her family includes two girls (affectionately nicknamed Yogi and Boo Boo). Papa Bear works for the fire department; he met Dana doing a dinner theater production of *The Velveteen Rabbit.* Ironically, their parts were husband and wife.

Dana is a 2009 American Christian Fiction Writers Book of the Year finalist for romantic suspense and an award winner in the Pacific Northwest Writers Literary Contest. Her novel *Betrayal in the Badlands* won a 2010 *RT Book Reviews* Reviewers' Choice Award. She has enjoyed writing a mystery series for Barbour Books and more than ten novels to date for the Love Inspired Suspense line.

She spent her college years competing in speech and debate tournaments all around the country. Besides writing, she busies herself teaching elementary school and reviewing books for her blog. Mostly, she loves to be home with her family, including a dog with social-anxiety problems, a chubby box turtle and a quirky parakeet.

Dana loves to hear from her readers via her website, at www.danamentink.com.

RACE FOR THE GOLD

DANA MENTINK

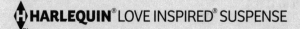
HARLEQUIN® LOVE INSPIRED® SUSPENSE

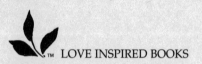

Recycling programs
for this product may
not exist in your area.

LOVE INSPIRED BOOKS

ISBN-13: 978-0-373-04192-3

RACE FOR THE GOLD

www.Harlequin.com

Printed in U.S.A.

These trials are only to test your faith, to show that it is strong and pure. It is being tested as fire tests and purifies gold—and your faith is far more precious to God than mere gold. So if your faith remains strong after being tried by fiery trials, it will bring you much praise and glory and honor on the day when Jesus Christ is revealed to the whole world.

—*1 Peter* 1:7

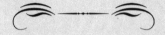

To Sugar Todd and all the athletes
who pour their heart and souls into their sport
and elevate us all in the process.

PROLOGUE

World Short-Track Speed Skating Qualifiers

The after-race recuperation did not sting quite as badly today; it was as if her muscles had gotten the news, the glorious golden news. Laney Thompson, gangly underdog in the short-track skating world, had just secured a spot on the American team. She was going to compete on the biggest stage in sports. It was an opportunity that only came around once every four years. Outside the speed skating arena where she'd spent the past two years of her life, the freezing air did nothing to cool the warm crackle of triumph that burned in her belly.

Max Blanco was next to her, suited up for their celebratory cooldown run along the road freshly cleared by a snowplow. She knew his elation matched her own. On a whim, she held a pretend microphone in front of his face, strands of her blond bob whipping against her cheek. "So, Mr. Max Blanco, how exactly does it feel to know you'll be going after the most important gold medal in speed skating a few months from now?"

He laughed and she tried not to fall too deeply into those aquamarine eyes that made something inside her dance like a wind-borne snowflake.

"Maybe I should be asking you that," he said. "How does it feel?"

She held her head up to the sky, closed her eyes and let the dancing flakes pepper her cheeks. "It feels like there is nothing in the world I can't do."

He suddenly grabbed her around the middle and swung her in dizzying circles until she was gasping for air.

"I told you, didn't I? You struggled all season, but you laid it down when it counted and now you're going. All the way!" He returned her to earth. "So after our run are you going to let me take you on a date?"

She felt herself blushing deeply. "We're together all the time."

He fisted hands on his lean hips and clucked. "That's called training, Laney. A date is when two people go out and have a good time together without the need for free weights and treadmills." He moved closer. "Come on, you promised once the trials were over you'd go out with me. I want to say I dated you before you won your gold."

She shivered. "Aren't you getting ahead of yourself?"

He toyed with a section of her hair. "It's only great if you've got someone to share it with, someone who understands."

Did she understand what drove him? She knew the nuts and bolts of short-track speed skating, she understood the drive, the fiery burn that propelled them all to work through pain, to compete with only one goal in mind. But though Max fascinated and attracted her, she did not fully understand him.

A few people filtered out of the arena, techie types mostly. Most of the athletes and trainers had gone home to celebrate or indulge their sorrows. That was the hardest part. Only six of her women friends on the National Team had made it and the rest were devastated, plain and simple. But that was short track. Friendships were left at the edge of the ice.

Max pulled a small envelope from the pocket of his nylon jacket, fiddling with the corners. "Here," he said, thrusting it into her hands.

She eased the flap of the envelope open and gently removed a tiny square of paper, notched and cut in what seemed like a million places. "What is it?" she breathed.

He took it from her hands and unfolded the square. It opened into the most intricate paper cutting she'd ever seen. He held it up and the sun shone through the minuscule cuts to reveal a bird, wings tucked, soaring against a cloud, breeze fluttering the paper feathers.

"That's the most beautiful thing I've ever seen." She'd watched him sometimes, sitting alone, scissors in his hand that he immediately put away when she approached.

He shrugged and folded it back up and

replaced it in the envelope. "A hobby of mine. Learned it when I was a kid."

She clutched the envelope to her chest. "I'm going to keep it forever."

"I think of you that way." He cleared his throat. "When you're racing, you're like a bird, flying over the ice without really touching it."

She found herself speechless as she tucked the little envelope carefully into her pocket. She knew where it would go every race, zipped under her skin suit, right next to her heart. "Thank you," she managed. "I love it."

He bent and fiddled with the lace on his shoe. "Ready to go, then?"

She nodded. "I'll let you lead, since that's what you're used to."

Laughing, sapphire eyes reflecting the sparkling snow, he headed up the road at an easy pace. They ran and laughed and dreamed together until five miles later they found they had looped back to the final bend in the road. Her fingers found the little envelope and she took it out again.

In his eyes, she was a bird, soaring, flying. The image hovered in her heart and awakened something she'd never felt before.

As if in some silent agreement, their pace slowed, breath puffing in the twilight, savoring the last portion of the run together. When they stopped, he took her in his arms again and she stared into those eyes now darkened by the shadows but still luminous as if they generated their own light from deep down in his soul.

He pressed his lips to her temple and she was lost in the warmth, the feel of his strong arms folded around her. "Congrats again, Laney. I know how you've struggled for this."

"We both have," she murmured.

Neither one of them heard the sound at first. The roar of an engine, the crunching of tires trying to find traction on the snow.

He broke off the kiss as the car rounded the corner, his hand clutching hers.

A flash of metal, the barest glimpse of the driver's face.

With a sickening crunch, the car plowed

into them. As she fell into the crisp layer of snow, she watched the tiny envelope settle gently to the ground.

ONE

Four long years, and it was as if the shock of the accident still lingered in her muscles, weakening the certainty she'd felt as a twenty-three-year-old champion. Now, at almost twenty-seven years old, Laney felt the eyes following her as she climbed from the heat box and clumped her way to the ice. Taking off her skate guards, she slid onto the sparkling surface of the ice and headed for the start line.

Was it whispers she heard from the coaches and the other girls? Or was it her own thoughts bubbling up to the surface, memories from four years before when she'd had her dream and lost it? It wasn't the venue that sparked the tension inside; she'd spent most of the past year training in this very spot. Nor was it the fear of losing, not really.

Though it was a practice race, it was an important one, an indication of her prospects for placing in the trials in a matter of weeks, the event that would decide who made the team for the Olympic Games.

Up until now she'd been training mostly on her own with Max, grinding her body back into shape in spite of the pain. Today was the time she would answer the question publicly. Was Laney Thompson back?

As she glided slow circles on the ice, she pondered the question she'd tried to answer for herself every day since the accident that broke her ankle and left her with a brain injury. Did Laney Thompson still have what it took to compete for the United States in the biggest meet of her life? Her competitions throughout the season had not been stellar, moments of brilliance mixed in with enough mistakes to leave room for doubt.

Again the tickle of guilt that inevitably came with the question. Did she even deserve to be back, poised for a second chance, when Max was not?

She knew he was there somewhere in the arena. How did he feel at that moment? Now a trainer, thanks to the screws in a hip that had been extremely slow to heal, he watched others strive to live out a passion now denied to him.

He'd emerged from the accident scarred inside, too, hidden damage that had caused him to withdraw from her. Or maybe he'd lost any tender feelings for her when she woke up unable to remember chunks of their time together. Something broke there on the snow that day, something more than bones and dreams. She didn't understand what it was, and maybe she never would.

Beth Morrison gave her a smile, dimples standing out against her pale face, dark hair sporting a hot pink streak today. The girl looked so incredibly young. And when, Laney thought drily, had she become the old lady of the team at almost twenty-seven years old? Beth pointed to Laney's left skate. "Not tight," she mouthed.

Laney blushed and dropped to a knee to try it again. Gifted athlete, natural dancer, all-around high achiever Laney Thompson still had to remind herself of the steps to tying her skates. Why had the nuances of short-track speed skating lingered in her memory, but the act of tying her laces remained a challenge? And reading a clock, and remembering to eat or what not to eat? She'd almost triggered an allergic reaction two days prior when she'd been ready to eat a nutrition bar containing peanuts. *It's the brain injury, Laney, not you.*

Tanya Crowley shot her an odd look before she concealed her eyes behind racing glasses. Was it disdain Laney saw on her lips? Mind games, an athlete's trick.

Laney wondered what would happen if she produced a terrible race here today. Practice or not, she knew her performance would answer the question in her own mind. Could Laney Thompson be the person she was before the hit-and-run driver had almost taken away her future?

Her eyes scanned the darkened arena for Max. She did not see him. Zipping her skin suit up to her neck, she had a flash of memory, picturing the cut paper bird he had given her a moment before their lives were changed. After the crash, he'd retreated so far she doubted if there ever really had been the sweet connection between them.

You're like a bird, flying over the ice without really touching it. Had she read more into those words than she should have?

Would he ever see her that way again? Or was she someone flying away with a dream that should have been his?

No more time to think about it, Laney. Get into position. Game face on.

Max stood in the shadows, his body tensing just as it always did before the start of a race. Practice run or the real thing, it had never made a difference. When the buzzer sounded, there was only the ice and the finish line and seventeen-and-a-half-inch blades carrying him to victory. That's what he had loved about it most, how racing stripped everything away to that simple equation. Insane levels of training plus a helping of talent equaled a win.

At least, it used to. He eased the weight off his bad hip, still stiff in spite of the massive efforts he'd made to rehab. It wasn't enough. He wasn't enough. The only thing that saved him from total despair was this job, the chance to help Laney achieve what they'd both lost. He wouldn't get all of it back. Anger twisted his soul into an impenetrable knot that separated him from everyone, even Laney.

He found his hands were clenched around the rail as he watched her get into the zone. Would she remember to focus on her cornering? He was already taking notes about her tendency to chat with the other girls. Always kindling with energy, Laney struggled with brain trauma that had left her with a shortened attention span. There was more riding on this practice run than anyone knew, except maybe him and Dan Thompson, Laney's foster dad, who paced anxiously up and down the opposite side of the oval.

He felt someone next to him. Jackie Brewster, Beth's coach, stood there with her impeccably perfect posture and gleaming silver hair. Coach Stan Chung was the lead coach of the U.S. national team, overseeing all the girls, but most competitors like Beth had the means to employ private ones.

"Does Laney have it together?"

"Absolutely," he said, bobbing his chin at Jackie's athlete. "And Beth looks like she's in good form."

Jackie nodded without taking her eyes off her own skater. "At this point, it's all mental, as we both know." She paused. "There is a gentleman hanging around out front, asking for Laney."

"What gentleman?"

She shrugged. "He said he's a reporter. I told him he could be the King of Siam and he wasn't going to get into the arena without an appointment."

Max nodded. "Thanks. She doesn't need any distractions right now."

"This is true. Security is lax around here. I already shooed away a kid who was hanging around last night."

Max had seen him, too, a skinny red-haired kid with a sweatshirt too small for him.

"See you after the race." Jackie patted him on the arm and went to take her place on the ice, stopwatch in hand, creased slacks an odd contrast to her clunky skate-clad feet. She was the only person he knew who could walk gracefully in skates.

Max saw Laney get into position. It was time for her to prove to herself that she had that heart of a lion, the ability to put everything and everyone out of her mind and go as fast and hard as she could for the five hundred meters it would take to win.

After some last-minute activity, the coaches took their places and everything went quiet. Max tensed with Laney as she raised her arm in front of her and crouched low, her blade tip dug into the ice. He realized he was taking slow, measured breaths, the same way she would be doing, bringing her mind into focus, preparing her muscles for the grueling challenge.

The bell sounded and Laney exploded from the start line so quickly she was a blur. After the initial chopping steps, she settled in to longer pushes, tucking into second position, the place where she was most comfortable as she waited to break away for the win. She leaned forward in the perfect crouch, gloved fingers skimming the ice as she rounded the turn, hands folded behind her on the straightaway.

"You've got this, Laney," he whispered.

"Are you Max Blanco?"

Max jerked. He'd been so intent on Laney that he hadn't noticed the lanky man come up next to him. "Who are you?"

The stranger regarded Max seriously, chewing on his thick mustache. "I asked you first."

Max scanned his shirtfront and found no identification tags. "You have permission to be in here?"

He smiled, one eye drooping slightly. "It's skating, not a nuclear missile test."

Max looked back at the ice. "What do you want?"

"A story."

Max offered him a momentary glance. "I'm busy."

"I want a story about Laney."

"She's busy, too."

"I'm patient. I can wait."

Max rounded on him then. "Look, man. Laney's racing, if you can't tell. She needs to concentrate, and so do I. Call and make an appointment like everyone else."

"I've called. No reply from any of the people I've tried. Almost like someone doesn't want me to talk to her."

Max looked at Laney as she completed another turn and he saw something there, something hesitant, a tiny flicker of uncertainty that was probably only visible to him. Instinctively, he moved for the entrance to the ice, eyes riveted on her.

The man took Max's arm. "I'm writing about the American team hopefuls. Want to follow a skater from here all the way through the Winter Games."

Max shook off the touch. "Good for you. Call again. Maybe you'll get an appointment."

"Maybe I'll stay and talk to her anyway."

With effort, Max controlled his rising temper. "Get out," he said over his shoulder as moved.

The man shrugged. "All right, but you're not her keeper off the ice."

"What's that supposed to mean?" Max received no answer as the guy ambled in the direction of the exit. Max knew he should follow and make sure the man was truly leaving, but he could not walk away, not then, with Laney skating this critical race, her sides heaving with the effort, bits of ice exploding from under her blades as she rounded the turn with two laps to go.

Tanya was in first position but fading, he could tell. Beth was in third, looking for the gap on the inside to pass Laney. From his perspective the skaters were packed together, but he knew they would see it differently, waiting for an opening, that fraction of space to slip into that would change everything.

And then, as if in slow motion, things did change.

Something upset the dynamic of the flying pack.

Laney spiraled out of control.

She felt the blade give slightly under her right boot, but there was nothing she could do to stop her momentum. The break in the rhythm, an odd shift of her weight over her forward skate told her brain what her body already knew: a crash was coming.

At forty miles per hour the only result of skidding out was hitting the wall. Hard.

Even cushioned by the thick blue pads, it was going to hurt. She prayed she could keep from taking out any of the other skaters or cutting herself open with her razor-sharp blades. In a blur of motion she went down on her right hip and slid at breakneck speed, the wall coming at her. One second more and she crashed into the pads, helmet first.

The impact knocked the wind out of her and she felt the pain of bones hitting ice; the recoil bounced her off the pads and sent her limbs spiraling in an unruly tumble. For a moment, there was only the harsh sound of her own breathing; the arena noises all faded away as she spun helplessly on her back. When her vision cleared, she was looking up at the ceiling of the oval, sparks dancing in front of her eyes. She lay still, feeling the shock of the impact shuddering through her body as she sucked in deep lungfuls of oxygen before she tried to move. Then Coach Stan was there, peering down at her, and behind him, Max's anxious face.

"Laney?" Coach Stan asked.

She realized what he wanted to know, but

she wasn't sure herself if she was injured or not. Max squeezed her hand. "Hey, Birdie. Tell me how you feel."

She closed her eyes. Birdie. The nickname tickled something inside her. She forced her eyelids open and managed a grin. "I guess the eagle has landed, but not very gracefully."

The coach seemed to relax a little, and Max squeezed one more time before he let go and the team medic took his place. She was checked and helped to her feet. Looking back across the ice, she was in time to see the racers finish, Tanya first, Beth in second place. Beth glided to them, chest heaving, along with the other girls.

"Are you okay?" she puffed. "What happened?"

"Dunno," Laney said as she made her way to the edge of the ice, put the guards over her skate blades and sat heavily on the wooden bench. Her father materialized there, and she knew that though he'd probably wanted to run right down on that ice, he would never have done so.

He clutched her around the shoulders, and

she felt his heartbeat vibrating through his skinny chest. When had he lost so much weight?

"Baby girl, you know how to crash with style," he said.

She laughed again, though it set off some pain in her rib cage.

"What hurts?" He asked it in that soft voice that always soothed her.

He'd asked when she'd come home from school in tears because the grade-school kids had found out her mother had abandoned them. He'd crooned it when years later she got a fat lip defending her younger sister from the unwanted attention of some teen thugs. He'd repeated it when she'd lain in a hospital bed crying for something she could not name. The loss of her chance at gold? The grief at knowing Max was suffering his own agonizing recovery? Or something else that would not come clear in her pain-fogged mind?

"Knee and elbow, ribs," she said, ticking off the list. "That about covers it." She looked to Coach Stan. "What now?"

"Now you rest up. Medic will check you out more thoroughly in a bit. Tomorrow we have a twelve-hour training day if you're up for it."

"I am."

He smiled. "I thought you'd say that. We'll do another practice race at the end of the week. Tonight you take it easy and let us know if you have any confusion."

"More than usual, you mean," Laney said.

Coach Stan patted her hand. "When you catch your breath, we'll talk it through, look at your dad's tapes."

Her father nodded and held up the video camera that he was never without. "Got it all right here."

Coach Stan made more notes on his clipboard and turned to talk to another trainer. "All right everybody. Change and we'll meet up for dinner in a half hour." And that was that. He hadn't posed the real question. Was she strong enough to win races and compete the following week to snatch at spot at the Winter Games?

For now, she would have to be content to wait. She pulled off the hood of her skin suit and unzipped it a few inches to cool her overheated muscles. Unlacing the boots, she took off the skates and put them in her bag. Max stood a few feet away, arms folded, brows drawn together under a shock of black hair that he'd let grow too long. She kissed her father. "I'm okay. I'll see you at dinner."

The girls from the race had collected on the nearby benches, removing their skates and discussing their own performances, cheeks pink from exertion, coaches and trainers mingling about. Tanya whispered something to Beth. Laney made her painful way to Max and they strolled to a quiet corner, both gazing out across the ice.

He looked at her closely. "I was tracking you, Laney. The race was pitch perfect until you made the second turn. What happened?"

She shrugged. "I don't know. Something felt off in my right skate."

There was an accusatory glint in his sapphire eyes.

"What?" she demanded.

"Sure you didn't lose your focus?"

"Yes, I'm sure. It was the skate."

He frowned.

"All right, spill it," she said, half-playfully. "You don't believe me?"

"I do," he said after a long moment. "But we've been having trouble with your concentration, and your skates haven't bothered you at all recently." He blew out a breath. "It's all up here," he said, tapping his head. "You've got to put yourself in the zone and stay there."

A small flame licked at her stomach, and her playful mood was gone. "I was in the zone, fully focused and with my game brain on. It was the skate."

The girls turned their faces in Laney's direction as they got up and left the arena, headed for their quarters. Coach Jackie gave them a curious glance before she shuttled Beth along, helping tote her gear. Laney allowed Max to put his arm around her shoulder, annoyed that his touch made something happen to her breathing.

"I understand what you've been through better than anyone else," Max said in low tones. "But you've got to push through that and deliver. The past has to remain on the benches when it's race time."

She saw herself reflected in the blue depths of his eyes, her outline blurred and morphed into a different shape. "Max," she said, pulling away a step, "I'm not you, so don't put your stuff on me."

His mouth thinned. "I'm talking as your trainer, Laney. That's all."

"And you don't think I'm focused enough because of what happened years ago?"

"I don't know. I'm trying to get inside your head."

"The problem isn't in my head for once, it's in my skate, so you should focus on that."

"I'm going to tell you what you need to hear to win, whether you want to listen or not," he snapped. "That's what your father pays me to do."

She knew from the anger kindling in his voice that she'd pushed back too much. It was true, she had struggled with focus throughout the season and his assumption about her performance today was understandable. She sighed. "I know you're trying to correct a mistake here, but I didn't make it, not this time. It was the skate." She hated the way that sounded like a lame excuse. Blaming the equipment was for rookies.

"All right," he said, wide shoulders stiff. "Let's take a look."

She returned to the bench and found her gear bag. She fished out the left skate and handed it to him, reaching into the bag for the other. It took two seconds for her to make sense of it. "My right skate is gone."

Max helped her hunt under the benches and in every darkened crevice. There was no sign of the missing skate.

"One of the girls must have picked mine up by accident."

Max raised an eyebrow. "No way. Not this level of athlete."

He was right. Speed skaters relied on their equipment like world-class musicians cherished their instruments. They didn't take the wrong skate accidently. Practical joke by Tanya or Beth or any of the other girls? She couldn't imagine it.

Laney felt at an utter loss. "How could it have walked away on its own?"

"It couldn't," Max said, blue eyes gone dark in the gloom. "Someone made it disappear."

TWO

Max reported the missing skate, and a full complement of coaches and competitors returned to scour the arena.

Beth flipped back her sleek bob of hair. "This is ridiculous. Laney, did you go anywhere? To the bathroom or something and leave it there?"

Laney's cheeks flushed pink. Max realized that the result of Laney's brain injuries was more public than he had known.

"She was here talking to me the whole time," he said.

Beth skewered him with a look. "So what you're implying is someone stole her skate? What would be the point, exactly? To cut her out of the competition?" She laughed. "Sorry, Laney, but we're not that scared of you. At least I'm not."

Max would have let her have it, but Laney giggled.

"You should be. I'm ferocious, didn't you know that?"

Beth grinned. "Yeah, that's you. Ferocious. Still sleep with your night-light on?"

"Of course. Keeps the monsters away."

Max marveled at Laney's easy smile, the positive glow in all circumstances that puzzled him. She should be a gold medalist already—she had the skill, the natural gift and the work ethic to match, and yet he could not find resentment in her face, the resentment that was so alive in his own soul.

Jackie finished her examination of the top tier of seats and returned. "There is no sign of it." Her eyes scanned the arena thoughtfully.

"What are you thinking?" Max asked.

"Nothing, I'm sure. I was just considering that there are no strangers here, the girls, the coaches, the trainers, the custodians. No strangers..."

He finished her thought. "Except the guy who wanted to talk to Laney."

"Who?" Laney asked.

"A reporter," Jackie said with disdain. "I told him to leave."

"So did I," Max said. "But I didn't actually see him go, did you?"

Jackie shook her head solemnly. "I was down on the ice, timing Beth. But what reason would he have for taking her skate?"

"Not one that I can think of," Max muttered.

Beth wrapped an arm around Laney. "You have spare skates?"

"She's got other pairs," Max said.

Beth gave him a sassy smile. "Yeah, I figured. Just thought I'd see if she needed to borrow temporarily or something." She followed her coach through the exit.

Laney sighed. "That was nice."

Nice? Max wondered. Or patronizing? Top-quality speed skates for skaters at this level were custom-made, the boots constructed using molds of the skater's feet, and there was no possible way for Laney to skate any kind of a race wearing borrowed gear. Beth knew that as well as he did. She also knew they cost upward of three thousand dollars a pair.

Laney's father, Dan, was footing the bill for her training time, equipment, coaching and Max's services. Something skittered through Max's stomach as he considered it might be a real hardship to find the money for another pair of skates. He resolved to talk to Dan Thompson...soon.

Laney changed and met Max outside. The air was cold, and they blinked to adjust to the darkness. Laney still simmered with annoyance. She wasn't making excuses and she hadn't misplaced her own skate, as the girls suggested. She wasn't *that* addled by her brain injury.

To their left was a parking lot that would be jammed when the public-skating hours commenced on the weekend. Now there were only a few cars, one of which was her father's banged-up Suburban.

"I'm..." she started when the crash of glass made her jump. Her father's rear window fractured, pieces glittering in the moonlight.

Laney raced to the vehicle, Max a few paces behind her. She found her father crouched on the other side of the car, arm raised to his face as a squat, bushy-haired stranger readied a club to crash into her father's skull. The stranger's face was partially obscured by a cap.

"No!" she shouted, surprising the man with the club. He swiveled quickly, swinging the weapon in an arc toward Laney. With reflexes born of elite levels of training, she ducked under the blow.

The club fell viciously, whistling by her ear, causing her to fall back against the car while the weapon smashed into the passenger door, crumpling the metal.

With an animal roar, Max went after the guy, who whirled on his heel and ran, Max in hot pursuit. Laney sprang to her feet, not sure if she should chase after Max or stay with her father.

"Laney," he croaked. "Keep out of it."

"Daddy," she breathed, eyes filling as she crouched next to him. "Are you hurt?"

"Just a knock on my thick head. Your mum always told me I had a hard skull."

Laney's stomach twisted in agony as she strained to catch a glimpse of Max. What would happen if he caught the guy? Squeezing her father's hand to comfort him, she felt the heavy thud of her pulse in her throat.

Finally, Max returned, panting.

"I lost him. I'll call the cops."

"No," her father barked.

Laney's mouth dropped open. "The guy could have killed you."

"He was a thief, wanted the iPad I left in the back probably. My own dumb fault."

Max dropped to one knee. "Mr. Thompson, the cops really should be notified, and the security team here at the oval."

"No cops," he repeated again, getting to his feet with Laney's help. "No harm done except a broken window and a dent, the price for my stupidity."

"But, Dad…"

He waved a hand. "I'll go inside and report it to security, but no cops. Not necessary. Now go on back to the dorms before you get a chill."

"I don't want you out here by yourself," Laney said as severely as she could.

"I'll have someone from security to walk me back. Go, go," he said with a flap of his hands. He bent with a groan and picked up his bag.

Laney was grateful when Max put his arm around her. His touch was the only thing that seemed to push away the cold that seized her from the inside out.

She was almost sure that she'd seen a glimpse of her father's iPad tucked safely in his bag before he left.

The distance from the oval to the athlete housing was a mile, which Laney and Max traversed in silence. Reaching the dorms, he used his pass key and held the door for her. Laney had been fortunate to be assigned her own room in the dormitory on the bottom floor where the female athletes and coaches stayed. Max was in another dorm with the male trainers, coaches and athletes. He waited while she opened her door, greeting her old cat, Cubby, whom she never traveled without, if possible.

"Thanks for walking me back."

"Anytime." He cleared his throat. "I feel

bad about what happened to your father, that I couldn't catch the guy."

She shivered. "Dad could have been hurt badly."

"And you, too," he added, feeling again the chill that had swept his body as the man's club had come within inches of her.

"I hope security can help."

"Strange how he targeted your dad's car. There were plenty of fancier models parked close by."

"He said the man was after his iPad." She looked away.

"But you don't believe that?"

She shook her head. "I'm really tired. Gonna rest for a little while."

"Good idea." He paused. "You know, Laney, you really were skating an excellent race."

She raised an eyebrow. "Except for that bashing into the wall thing?"

He couldn't help it, the wry expression on her face made him laugh, and she joined in. Then he grabbed her for a quick hug, pressing her fiercely as if he could push away the edge in his earlier words. "I'm sorry if I sounded like I didn't believe you about the skates."

She rested her head on his chest. "It's okay. I can take it. I'm ferocious, remember?"

He thumbed her chin up and shook his head at that easy smile, the gleeful twist of the lips that carried her through every situation. "Definitely," he said. The urge seized him to stroke that tumble of hair and press his lips to the silk of her cheeks. *Knock it off, Blanco. That life is long gone.* It had ended when he'd woken up in a hospital bed, irretrievably broken and with an unquenchable anger that he did not want Laney to witness. Ever. He'd hidden himself away from her, from the world, not allowing himself to consider the feelings he'd cherished once upon a time. He stepped back. "I'll see you at dinner."

She nodded and closed the door.

He was halfway down the hall when she opened the door again. "Max?"

He jogged back. "Yeah?"

She held a small, white rectangle between her fingers. "I guess that reporter really does want to speak with me. He wrote a note on his card saying he hoped I hadn't hurt myself today." She frowned at the paper. "He was watching the race. All of it."

Laney turned the reporter's name around in her mind again as she walked to the dining hall an hour later. Hugh Peterson. Had she ever spoken to him before? She did not think so, but somehow the name dinged a little bell in her memory. There had been many reporters anxious to talk to her before, when she was poised to go for the gold four years ago, and some had followed her progress for a while after the accident, but their interest had eventually died away. The tragic injury of a promising athlete was newsworthy; a long, painful rehab with no guarantee of success was not.

Max was troubled by Hugh's card more because of the fact that the man had been roaming the halls of the athletes' quarters unattended. Somehow he'd gained entry without a pass key. Laney figured it was typical reporter nosiness, though she was uncertain as to why Peterson wanted to speak to her. Sure, it would be a great comeback story, but she was far from any kind of victory. Most media types would wait until after the trials.

You're like a bird, tottering on the edge of the nest. You gonna fly or crash?

The image reminded her of the paper cut-out Max had made her so many years ago. How she wished she still had it, to remind herself of the tenderness he'd shown, the sweet, intense man who was so out of keeping with the brilliant short-track star. She shook the thoughts away as she entered the dining hall, saying hello to the benches full of girls, coaches, trainers and the nutritionist who greeted her with anxious inquiries about her health. Furtive looks indicated they'd heard about her father's incident in the parking lot.

Max was at the end of the table, a half-eaten chicken sandwich in front of him. Her father arrived, greeting everyone jovially, a bruise swelling his cheek as he settled in to listen intently to Max. She joined them.

"So this reporter really wants to speak to

Laney. Said he's called many times," Max finished. "Do you remember hearing from him?"

Her father frowned. "What's his name again?"

"Hugh Peterson," Laney said, sliding onto the bench in time to see her father clank the glass down on the table so hard he spilled a puddle onto the wooden surface.

She blinked. "You told him no before, I take it?"

"Yeah, I did. He doesn't listen very well."

"Have you met him, Dad?"

"He's no good," her father said vehemently.

"How do you know him, Mr. Thompson?"

Her father waved a hand. "Not important. I know I don't like him." He turned a direct gaze on Laney. "You're not to talk to him. He shouldn't have come here after I told him no interview."

The anger in his tone surprised her. "Why do you dislike him so much?"

"I already said that's not important. Do you trust me to manage these things for you or not, Laney?" He stood, pushing back from the table.

She went to him then, circling him in a hug. "Of course I trust you, Daddy. If you don't want me to talk to him, then I won't. I was just curious, that's all, and worried about that guy with the club who nearly decked you."

"Max scared him away. He won't be back." Her father embraced her gently and rubbed circles on her shoulders, soothing, restoring the easy connection between them. "I'm sorry, Laney. I didn't mean to bark at you. I just want to take care of my girls. That's all I've ever wanted to do."

She pressed a kiss to each of his cheeks. "I know that. Sit down and let's eat. I'm going to Skype Jen soon and we can talk. She's cramming for her biology finals now." Laney felt the thrill of pride that her little sister, who'd once been an abandoned foster kid, was close to finishing her premed requirements. It was an achievement for anyone, but more so for a girl whose life had started out living in cars and stepping over dirty needles on bathroom floors. Laney thought Jen's accomplishment outweighed any medal from any race.

He set her at arm's length. "Later. I've got to have the car window fixed."

"But…" She didn't want him out on his own in case he was wrong about the violent stranger.

"I'll be back." He gave her shoulder a final squeeze and made his way through the throng.

"Why don't you get something to eat?" Max said.

She shook her head. "I'm not hungry."

He pulled her to sit next to him. "A girl who burns five thousand calories in a day needs to eat. I'll get you something. Stay here."

She didn't argue. Her thoughts swirled around her father. Dan Thompson was not a man quick to anger. If anything, he'd been blessed with an abundance of patience and an overwhelming helping of compassion. An overworked cabbie, struggling to start his own small taxi business, he'd needed them in order to take in foster kids in the first place. It was a decision he and his wife Linda had made, having no children of their own. And what well of grace had made them take on two girls—a wild six-year-old kid with dirty hair, used to finding food for her and her sister in the garbage can when their mother left on her drug binges, and a selective mute who would not speak until she was nearly ten?

He could have walked away at any point. Perhaps when she'd taken Jen and ran away after being punished for punching the neighbor kid. Maybe when the teacher had sent her home for refusing to wear shoes in class. Certainly when Linda had died of breast cancer as they were still in the process of formally adopting the girls.

He'd stayed and loved them through it all, and introduced her to the ice. Stolen hours between his cab fares, precious moments where she'd discovered a passion and let go of the hurt. God-blessed moments. Her father's face was composed and calm as he stopped to make some comment to Jackie, and it cheered Laney to see him that way as he left. Maybe there really was nothing wrong, after all.

THREE

After dinner, Max dutifully made sure the hallway door was locked when he escorted Laney to her room. He turned to find her shifting from one foot to the other. He recognized the fidgets for what they were: Laney trying to process something: worry or fear, anxiety about her father's attack, no doubt.

So different than his own bent. When he was stewing on something he went quiet, withdrawing to a place where he could be perfectly still, hushed as the long corridors in which he'd become invisible seventeen years prior when his brother lay dying. The softest sound, the barest squeak of a rubber-soled shoe on those yellow hospital tiles could break the fragile silence that meant his brother was okay, sleeping peacefully through another night.

God worked in those still moments, he'd been told. So he'd stayed silent, waiting for healing that God withheld. Often Max would go back to that place in his mind, and his fingers would once again reach for his pocket for the tiny pair of scissors that was no longer there. He required stillness to wrestle with tensions he could not skate away from, but not Laney.

"Let's go walk the track."

She started, as if she hadn't realized he was still there. "What?"

"You aren't going to be able to sleep."

"How exactly do you know that?"

Because I know you almost better than you know yourself. Every sinew, every muscle, every weakness, every magnificent strength. "You're twisting."

She looked at her finger, wound in the string of her windbreaker. "Well…"

"And your foot is jiggling up and down, and you look like you're about ready to break into a wind sprint."

She flashed an exasperated grin. "Sometimes I wish you didn't know me so well."

"I'm your trainer. It's my job." *My job.* So

why did Laney Thompson feel like so much more than just his job?

"I'm just keyed up about what happened to Dad."

"I know." The hallway lighting picked up glints of gold in her hair, an irrepressible twinkle in her eyes.

"All right, Mr. Blanco. To the track we go."

Max waited at the door while Laney changed into her running shoes and fed Cubby his fish dinner. Cubby was a slow eater, and Max stood patiently as Laney watched to be sure the old animal finished every bite.

"Good job, Cubby Cat," she said as the cat licked his paws with a delicate tongue.

The night closed around them as they started away from the athlete housing, the sky pricked by numberless stars. To the left was a small trail that led to a lake now frozen over. They'd run it many times in years past when their training and competition schedule had brought them here. A delicate veil of snow drifted through the sky as they took the other direction, on a well-paved sidewalk that led to the training facility.

He wondered if she ever fought flashbacks of the night they'd been the victims of the hit-and-run driver. Though he'd never admit it, he hated to run anywhere in the vicinity of a road, preferring now to do his workouts on the track or on quiet mountain trails when he could find them. If he closed his eyes and allowed his mind to travel back, he could hear the skidding tires and the snapping of his own femur. Worst of all, he remembered hearing Laney cry out, his own body too mangled to allow him to claw through the snow to reach her. One quiet moan that would live forever in his memory.

He forced his brain back to the present as they hiked to the oval. He marveled again at the engineering feat required to build such a venue. Five acres, roughly the size of four football fields, nestled under a clear span suspension roof, home to a four-hundred-meter speed skating oval and two international-size ice sheets. Buried under the ice sheets and track were thirty-three miles of freeze tubes that kept the concrete base at eighteen degrees Fahrenheit no matter the season. They were headed now to the four-lane 442-meter state-of-the-art running track.

He ushered her in first, darting one more look at the serenely falling snow behind them. A movement caught his attention. Off near the tree line, under the shifting shadows. A person? He looked again. Nothing at first, making him think perhaps it was a raccoon or maybe a bird. As he started to turn away, a figure detached itself from the shadows and began moving toward the lake.

Probably someone out for a walk, not unusual, except that the person appeared to have come from the direction of the athlete housing. *So what?* he asked himself again. An athlete or trainer out for a stroll, nothing more, winding down just as they were. Nonetheless, prickles of unease danced along the back of Max's neck as he noticed that the person had a small bundle under one arm.

"Be right back," he called to Laney, and for some reason he could not explain he found himself following.

"Max?" Laney called from behind him. "Where are you going?"

He didn't answer. Walking quickly, he closed the gap.

Whoever it was didn't notice his approach until they were nearly to the wooden dock that served as an overlook and a cast-off point for fishermen trying their luck in the lake. The figure gave a surreptitious glance around, stealthy and unsettling.

"Hey," Max said.

The form jerked.

Max saw he'd been right—the stranger held a bundle in his arms, which he now readied himself to throw into the water.

"What are you doing?" Max said again.

He heard the sound of running feet and Laney sprinted into view. Max knew suddenly what was in that dark bundle, and he also knew he would not let it go to the bottom of the lake. He reached out to stop the outstretched hands, trying to seize the wrists.

Something sliced through his forearm in a sizzle of pain. He heard Laney cry out as he pitched backward into the water, the weight of his body punching through the thin crust of ice at the lake's edge.

* * *

Laney hadn't realized she was screaming as she ran. No words, just an explosion of emotion. Events unfolded in rapid-fire, just as they did in every race. The shove. Max crashing into the water, chips of ice spiraling upward luminous in the moonlight. Movement, darkness, an endless moment of fear.

Then Max's head popped up. The person who'd pushed him slipped, fell forward before getting up and running along the trail. She didn't think, just moved, muscles overriding good sense as she closed the gap and hurtled onto the shoulders of the person who had just shoved Max into the pond.

"What are you, crazy?" she grunted.

He, it was a man, she concluded quickly, was sturdy and strong and her fingers lost their grip on the slippery fabric of his ski jacket. She fell to one knee and the man wriggled out of her grasp, grabbed the bundle from the ground and sprinted away. She could run him down, she knew, but she was not sure she could restrain him.

Scrambling to her feet she turned to the water. "Max," she screamed as loud as she could.

Beth Morrison raced up, dressed in a warm jacket and jeans. "What…?" she started.

"In the pond," Laney said by way of an answer, yanking off her shoes.

"You're not jumping in there," Beth said, clutching Laney's arm.

Laney shrugged her off and made for the edge of the dock.

"No," Max shouted from the pond. "Laney, do not jump into this water," he hollered. "I'm okay."

She knew it was not true. At her feet was the proof. Drops of blood dotted the snow, and she was pretty sure whom it belonged to. She pushed to the edge of the dock.

"No, Laney. He's coming out," Beth said, grabbing her again. "Look."

Max was indeed making his way to the dock, swimming where he could until he reached the iced edge and then cracking his way through. "He needs help," she said. "He's got a bad hip."

Jackie Brewster hurried up, her cheeks pink, breathing hard. "He's perfectly fit, and you are not to go in that water, either one of you," she commanded, unzipping her jacket. "I will if necessary."

"He's my trainer…" Laney began. *Friend. Confidant. The one who knows me best,* her heart filled in. She hesitated, body leaning toward Max, jaw clenched.

"Exactly why he does not want his world-class athlete diving into freezing water," Jackie snapped.

They stared, riveted, tracking Max's progress as he swam laboriously to within several feet of the dock.

Laney dropped to her stomach and stretched out her hands to him, her torso hanging over the wooden slats.

"You're going to fall in," Beth said, clutching Laney's legs.

"And so are you," Jackie added, grabbing Beth around the waist.

Laney snatched up Max's wrist. She could see pain rippling across his face along with the determination.

"Don't, Laney," he said tightly. "Your shoulder. I'll get out myself."

He referred to the shoulder she'd dislocated while weight training six months before. "My shoulder is fine, and if you don't take my hand I'll jump in and shove you out."

The muscles in his jaw worked overtime but he clasped her palm.

Together the three of them managed to haul Max out of the frigid water and up onto the dock where he sat, his knees shivering.

Laney put her hands on his shoulders. "Max?"

"Don't get wet," he said. "Either one of you. I don't want anybody…"

"Catching pneumonia," Laney finished. "I know, I know." In spite of his commands, she took hold of his arm. "We're getting you inside."

He climbed to his feet and shook off the assistance. He gripped his forearm.

"Can you make it?" Laney asked, the darkness working against her as she tried to look him over.

"Of course," he growled. She probably should have taken offense at his tone, but she knew she would have answered the same way. The mind overrides the body. Mental toughness. They'd steeped themselves in it. Terrible patients, both of them.

They made it back to the athlete dorms and hustled him inside to the dining room. Laney snapped on the lights and Beth began a violent sneezing fit that earned her a worried look from Jackie. Laney ran to fetch a blanket that she draped around Max's shoulders.

"What happened?" she demanded. "I turned around and you were off chasing someone to the pond."

Blue lipped, Max took a corner of the blanket and applied pressure to his arm.

Laney pushed closer. "Bad?"

He shook his head, sending icy droplets flying.

Jackie frowned. "Did the man have a knife?"

"No." Max turned to Laney. "Do you have your phone? I need to call security."

She fished it out of her pocket and handed him the phone. "What happened? You have to tell me. Was it the same man from the parking lot?"

"Didn't see his face."

"Why...?"

He held up a calming hand the same way he always did when she wanted to be skating hard and fast and he forced her to stop and recuperate. *Think it through, Birdie,* was his never-ending mantra.

She was thinking it through, and the mental energy was getting her nowhere except to a state of near panic.

He tried to dial the phone, but his fingers shook too much so she took it and punched in the numbers before handing it back to him.

"I need to report a problem," he said before giving a cursory summary and hanging up. "They're on the way."

She was pacing now, short, frantic circles as she texted her father.

"Laney, sit down, please," he said, moving another chair closer. "With me."

She forced herself into the chair. "Why did you go after the guy in the first place? He was built like a brick wall."

He jerked. "How do you know that?"

She sighed. "I tried to tackle him."

His eyes widened and a tinge of color flooded his pale cheeks. "You...did what?"

Jackie gave him a weary nod. "That's what I thought, too."

He took her hand and squeezed it hard. "Dumb, Laney. I don't even have to say why, do I?" he asked in clipped tones.

"No, so don't bother. It was just as dumb as you taking on the guy and winding up in the lake."

"I'm…" Max broke off and blew out a hissing breath.

Laney shrugged. "Anyway, he got away and that's that. Why were you after him in the first place?"

Max heaved a deep sigh, reining in his temper she surmised.

"I saw someone down by the pond, ready to heave something into the water."

"And you didn't think it might be a good idea to let him chuck it in and then figure out what it was later?" Beth said, arms folded.

"I knew what it was and I didn't want it to get wet or trapped there when the rest of the lake froze over."

"Why?" Laney nearly shouted. "What was it?"

In the dim light his electric-blue eyes were

dark and flat. He leveled a look her way that pricked her nerves.

"I think it was your missing skate."

For a long, silent moment, they all stared at Max.

"Why," Laney started slowly, "would anyone want to toss my skate in the lake?"

Beth folded herself in a tight hug. "To hide the fact that they tampered with your blade."

The sound of approaching feet signaled the security team.

"It all sounds so cloak and dagger," Jackie said. "Are you sure, Max? Very sure?"

He pulled up the ruined sleeve of his running jacket, exposing the neat slice that bisected his arm. "Look like the mark of a seventeen-inch steel blade to you?"

Something cold and ugly slithered up Laney's spine. "That's exactly what it looks like," she whispered.

FOUR

The security people contacted the police, and Max went over the scenario all over again after he was allowed to pull on dry clothes. He'd refused the hospital trip, of course, knowing the wound did not require stitches, and allowed Jackie to patch him up with the first-aid kit. He'd been cut dozens of times in the course of his short-track career. It came with the territory.

The wound stung, not enough to bother him, but two details would not stop circling in his mind. First, someone had taken Laney's skate. Though the guy had somehow managed to pick up the bundle and take it with him, there was no question that someone wanted to get rid of the evidence. Dressed in dry clothes, holding a cup of hot tea at Laney's insistence, he felt cold through and through. Who would do something that might result in a racer getting seriously injured? Who wanted her to lose that much?

The second fact that ate at him was Laney's reckless move down by the pond. Maybe he'd been cavalier in his actions, too, but she was not allowed to be. He interrupted her pacing and pulled her to the corner of the dining room while an officer by the name of Bill Chen interviewed Beth and Jackie.

He remembered Chen's face from the dozens of interviews he'd done after he regained consciousness those painful years ago— the fringe of salt-and-pepper hair, the five o'clock shadow on the round chin no matter what time of day Chen showed up. The officer had been polite and patient, teasing out information as best he could in between Max's surgical procedures and periods of sedation.

It hadn't made any difference. No matter how many times Max had gone over the details of the accident, he could not describe what he hadn't seen in the first place, since his back had been to the car that hit them and he'd been lost in Laney's eyes just before his life was ruined.

"I don't know what's going on here," Max told her. "But you've got to promise me you're going to be smart and safe until we get it straightened out. Doors locked, don't leave your equipment out in the open."

"Don't take candy from strangers?"

"It's not funny," he snapped.

She cocked her head, mouth quirked in that way that showed the one small dimple in her cheek. "It looks bad, but really, I'm sure there's no one after me. Why would there be? I'm just not that important."

"I don't know, but I think someone damaged your skate and tried to cover it up."

She laughed. "That sounds like a bad TV movie. Who would bother?"

"Laney, for every gold medalist there are plenty of losers who would have done absolutely anything to win."

Her eyes widened. "You didn't used to be so cynical. When you lost, it was one race, one day. You didn't let it define you."

He shoved his fingers into his wet pockets, fingers automatically feeling for the scissors that weren't there, the ones he'd used to cut out little paper animals of every description, a hobby he'd acquired at seven years of age. "I didn't even get the chance to lose, and I'm angry about that. You should nurse a little anger, too. It will fuel you to the finish line."

"Then I don't want to be there." She trailed fingers along his arm. "I'm going to win because I've trained hard and I love the sport and I want it. But if I don't, I won't consider myself a loser." Her voice dropped to a whisper. "And I don't consider you one, either. Never have."

"It's not about me anymore, as you said. It's about you. You're going to get your chance to win that medal."

"And if I don't?" He could see the troubled curve to her lips, the heavy lashes that framed her eyes. "Will you see me as a loser, too?"

"No," he said, throat suddenly tight. "I would never think of you like that. Ever." *Laney, you could never be anything but amazing to me,* said the tender part inside him, the only part left that was any good.

"Then why don't you extend yourself the same courtesy?"

The words hung between them, and he could not think of a single proper way to put the twist of feelings in his gut into words. He reached out and took her by the shoulders. "Listen, this isn't a joke. You have to be careful."

"Because I'm your athlete, and you don't want me to get knocked out of competition again?"

He could not stand that hazel gaze, the unspoiled sweetness that he had no right to enjoy anymore. Swallowing hard, he nodded. "Yes. That's right."

She gave him a puzzled look. "Max, sometimes I think you forget that what we do isn't all that important in the scheme of things."

His stomach tensed. She was losing her motivation, the drive to win. Maybe he could have a buddy of his, a sports psychologist talk to her. "You've got…"

Now it was Laney who held up a calming hand. "Don't get me wrong, I want to win that spot on the team more than anyone else in this building, and I'm going to do that. I'm chasing that medal with everything in my possession, every ounce of talent and hard work that I can bring to bear. But what I do is skate fast. I'm not changing the world. They're just races. And, yes, I'm going to skate the fastest short-track races in history because that's what God made me to do, but racing is just one thing, one small part of who I am."

He could not understand why she looked happy, uncertainly poised as she was on the greatest competition threshold of her life, with someone trying to make sure she did not get there. All she did was skate fast? Just races? He blinked. "I don't get you sometimes. It wasn't a small part of my life when I had it. It was my whole life." *And it should be yours, too.*

"That's where you made your miscalculation, Mr. Blanco. You skated fast because that's what God made you to do, but that was just one heat."

He felt a flash of pain. "You can say that because you can still race." Suddenly he wanted to cut down her joy, to diminish that incomprehensible happiness from her face. "What will you do when it's over?"

She smiled, a big wide grin that seemed to light a candle in the depths of her pupils and ignite the shame deep down in his own gut.

"Then I'll find out what He wants me to do next."

He stood, agog, until she lifted on tiptoe and aimed a clumsy kiss that landed at the corner of his mouth. "I'm so relieved that you're all right. You are more to me than the man who will help me stand on top of the podium." Then, with the gentlest of caresses to his cheek, she moved away to greet her father.

He realized he was staring at her, so he gathered up his wits and joined Mr. Thompson, who listened to the whole story again, his face grave as the police finished their interviews and promised to check in the next day.

Laney reached a finger out and wiped at a grease stain from her father's chin. "What did you get into, Dad? Were you working on the cabs?"

He swiped as the smudge. "Yeah. Got a loose belt that needed attention."

"I thought Mike handled that for you."

Mr. Thompson rolled his shoulders. "We all pitch in."

Tanya emerged in the hallway, wrapped in a bathrobe, long brown hair neatly braided into two plaits. "What's all the noise? I was going to get a snack from the kitchen."

"In your track shoes?" Laney said.

Tanya looked down at her expensive trainers. "Since I stepped on a nail last season, I don't go anywhere in bare feet."

Beth and Jackie joined them and filled Tanya in on the events. Tanya poked a finger at Beth's shoulder. "How'd you get involved in this? And where'd you go? Thought we were going to watch a movie."

Max registered for the first time that Jackie and Beth were both dressed for going outside.

Beth waved a hand. "I wanted to talk to my boyfriend, Cy." Her eyes narrowed, shifting slightly to Jackie. "There's no privacy anywhere around here, so I went outside."

Jackie's lips thinned. "Arranging a meeting?"

"No," Beth shot back. "I don't want to

get grounded again for sneaking out," she snapped, words rich with sarcasm. "But I'm going to be twenty next week, and technically I'm a legal adult, and you're not my mother."

"You're far from an adult," Jackie said smoothly.

Beth flushed. Tanya took her by the arm. "Come back to the room and tell me what Cy said. I've got to live vicariously through you, you know, and the other girls are going to want to hear all about the skate-in-the-pond adventure."

"Ten o'clock lights out," Jackie said to their retreating backs. Neither girl turned to acknowledge the remark.

"Ten o'clock curfew," Jackie called again.

"I know, I know," Beth snapped.

"Then stop testing," Jackie said, matching Beth's volume and then some. "And don't forget what you're here for."

"Doesn't matter if I forget. You'll remind me," the girl said with bitterness before she allowed Tanya to lead her away.

Max could read nothing from Jackie's expression. "Were you checking up on her?"

Jackie gave him a blank look. "What?"

"You were outside, too, during the pond incident. Were you checking up on her?"

Jackie sighed, shadows of fatigue darkening her skin. "She's impulsive, immature. She needs a mother as much as a coach. I'm not very maternal." Jackie spoke as if she was talking to herself. "Her mother is the CEO of the biggest mining company in the world. She gave Beth everything, but you can't give somebody drive. You have to be hungry to have drive."

Max knew exactly where his own hunger had come from. It was born in the antiseptic waiting room where he'd taken off his shoes and practiced his wobbly skating skills on the linoleum while his four-year-old brother Robby had endured treatments for leukemia. The disease had taken his life anyway, a few days before his fifth birthday.

Lap after lap had buried the need deeper. He would control his own body to the point where he was the best in the world, invincible. His own parents had means, but Beth's mother had billions. And Laney's birth mother? She'd had the need only to feed her habit, from what he'd learned. Maybe Jackie was right; they both hungered in their own way. He was not sure what to say, and he saw from the uncomfortable look on Laney and Mr. Thompson's faces that they shared his unease.

"Beth's going to do well," Laney said softly. "She'll dig down deep to get what she wants."

"She wants a mother, not a coach," Jackie said, still gazing down the darkened hallway. "But she's not going to get that from me." Jackie shook her head and seemed to rouse herself from her thoughts. "I had four brothers."

"No kids?" Mr. Thompson asked.

She answered dreamily, "A son. He's a trial lawyer." She thumbed her phone to life and showed them the photo of a dark-haired, thick-browed man. "Lives with his dad. Fortunate for him, because mothers make their kids weak," she said with a glance at Laney. "You're better off without one."

Max saw Laney flinch, and he frowned at the massive insensitivity, but Coach Jackie appeared not to notice.

Mr. Thompson put an arm around Laney. "She did have a mother, a good woman who loved her enough to let her be who she was meant to be."

Jackie smiled. "And a father who didn't let the mother get in the way."

Dan's face tightened and he squeezed Laney closer as Jackie said good-night and left.

"She's harsh," Max said, trying to gauge Laney's reaction.

Laney broke into her customary smile. "Maybe we could learn from her." She put on her best scowl. "It's time for bed everyone. Especially all those who have recently jumped in freezing-cold ponds and such."

He chuckled. "You taking over my job?"

"Of course, so go take your supplements, drink eight glasses of water and get to sleep fast so you'll be your cheerful good self tomorrow at training."

"Is that an order, Laney?" he teased.

"Absolutely," she proclaimed, kissing her father, taking Max's arm and propelling him toward the exit.

Max allowed himself to be swept along in

the tide of Laney's cheerful conversation, but he knew she must be wondering, as he was, who had taken her skate and tried so hard to get rid of it.

As they walked past the windows, he had an uncomfortable feeling that there were more problems waiting in the darkness.

The gray predawn did nothing to lighten the tiny bathroom as Laney ruefully consulted the little notes she'd taped to the bathroom mirror reminding her which of the taps in the shower was for the hot water. Many a scalding she'd endured before she'd swallowed her pride and wrote the messages to herself. Hot and cold, only two choices and it frustrated her to no end that she could not remember that simple detail, one even a child could manage.

So you need a note, Laney. So what? The needles of hot water soothed her muscles, still sore from the crash. A slight pain in her shoulder reminded her that the day had gone from a crash to a tackle, which seemed hard to believe as she greeted another morning. Whatever had happened, she was determined not to let it deflect one iota of mental energy from her training. Run the day or it will run you, Max always told her.

Somehow the image of Max disappearing under the water stubbornly refused to leave her head. At the moment he sank, she had not cared about anything else in the world but that he should resurface unharmed. He was her trainer and friend, she reminded herself. Of course she would feel that way. But something new and different circled inside her chest, a feeling that she'd not experienced in a very long time, irregular and delicate as a bird hopping from branch to branch. She pressed her hands to the wet tile and tried to refocus.

There was one thing and one thing only that could drive every thought and care from her psyche, and that was training. Long, grueling, bone-crunching training. The surge of fire in her belly urged her on as she dressed and packed her gear for the oval. Her second pair of skates, her only other pair, was packed safely in her bag, along with the EpiPen she'd fortunately never had to use.

Needles, she thought with a shudder. A person could live a very happy life without ever having a close encounter with one. She'd had plenty after the hit-and-run accident. Cubby grudgingly awakened and ate his cat food topped with a small piece of chicken she'd swiped from the kitchen. In stealth mode, she let herself out, locking the door behind her.

The other doors along the hallway were closed. At 5:00 a.m., the girls would be clinging to those last few hours of sleep. No sound of anyone stirring, even Mama Love, the team chef, who she knew liked to get a good start on the breakfast preparations. Laney took an apple and a hard-boiled egg from the snack drawer in the fridge and let herself outside into the cold.

"Good morning."

She jumped a step backward from the security guard.

"You scared me."

He smiled politely. "Sorry. Checking on the dorms. Going out?"

She nodded. "To the ice."

"So early?"

"I like to start my day before everyone else."

"Guess that's the way champions are made." He offered to escort her.

"No, thanks...." she started, until she considered the tongue-lashing she'd get from both Max and her father for puttering around unattended in the solitary early-morning hours. "Actually, that would be great," she said, shouldering her gear.

They walked in silence and she slipped inside and took a deep breath, waving at the guard as he left. Though most people wouldn't agree, she knew ice had a smell and she savored it now, sucking in a deep lungful of air and letting it tingle through her as it might have done for all the world-class athletes who had trained in this very spot.

She made her way past the bleachers toward the multilane track that circled the rink, planning an easy run to warm up, but the familiar sound of blades skimming the ice stopped her.

Max was alone on the ice, blade positioned,

arm crooked in front of him, focused. His form was perfect, balanced and contained, ready to explode from the start line. Her stomach clenched as she watched. One second and the imaginary buzzer must have signaled his mind because he propelled himself forward and shot across the ice.

He went hard for several meters, then drifted into a glide. She could see what others wouldn't, the tightness in his left leg that prevented him from cornering properly, his crouch not quite low enough, not quite there.

His head dropped along with her heart, and she knew he came here when no one else was around so they wouldn't see Blaze, former world-class competitor, struggling to complete a turn properly. She drew back into the shadow of the bleachers to allow him his dignity.

Lord, let him see he's meant to be more.

FIVE

Laney did not hear Hugh Peterson move next to her until he cleared his throat.

"What are you doing here?" she demanded. "Sneaking around like you did when you left your card under my door?"

"Not sneaking, looking for you."

"You're not supposed to be here." She shot a look toward Max.

"Why? He's here, and he's not even a competitor. Not like I'm going to steal any training tips."

Her teeth ground together. "He's my trainer, and you don't have a right to spy on him or anyone else."

The reporter's hair was graying at the temples, the skin around his eyes puckered, as if he'd spent plenty of time in the sun, but she guessed he was no more than mid-sixties.

He was dark complexioned, and his mustache completely obscured his upper lip. "You folks are a little too impressed by your own importance. I'm just here to talk to you. I tried calling and leaving messages. Most normal people would respond via those avenues."

"I didn't get any messages."

"Then you shouldn't leave your father in charge. I'd have called you directly, but he wouldn't give me your number."

"I'm glad he didn't," she said, though something squeezed uncomfortably inside. "What do you want, anyway?"

"I freelance for some sports mags." He pulled out a ragged spiral notepad from the back pocket of his baggy jeans. "I want an interview."

"Why not wait until after the trials? You might be wasting your time on me."

He smiled, but there was no amusement in his eyes. "You suffered a tragic accident four years ago that took away your dreams of gold."

Not just mine. She stayed silent.

"So you're a comeback kid."

"We're a long way from that."

He shrugged. "Tell me about the accident."

Flickers of worry flamed to life. At first she'd tried so hard to remember the faces, the driver, the make of the car, but her brain stubbornly kept the details cloaked in darkness. After many years she'd come to realize it was a blessing. She would not have to replay those horrifying moments in her mind over and over. "That's behind me, and I want to keep it that way." She shot a glance at the ice. Max was no longer visible from her line of sight, which gave her a queasy feeling.

"Just a couple of questions, that's all," he said. "I know you told the cops you didn't remember the driver, but did you get a sense, any indication at all that it was a man or woman driving?"

"No."

"Come on." He stepped closer. "You had to have some idea."

"I don't," she said, cold prickling her spine.

"I heard someone messed up your skate and tried to hide the evidence."

The bleachers pressed uncomfortably into

her back. "What does that have to do with the accident?"

He moved closer now, until she could smell coffee on his breath. "Could be it has everything to do with it. Name Trevor Ancho mean anything to you?"

"No. Should it?"

A bead of sweat rolled down her temple. "The things you're saying, they don't sound like regular interview questions, Mr. Peterson."

He shrugged. "I'm surprised at your reluctance, here. Seems like a kid would want to attract some attention, maybe garner a new sponsor to help Daddy pay all those bills."

"What do you know about my father?"

"I know he's in a financial hole, and he's made some crazy choices to continue bankrolling your dreams."

"What choices?"

"Let me interview you. We'll talk."

"I get the feeling you have an agenda that has nothing to do with my speed skating."

He stepped closer. "There's a lot more going on here than what happens on the ice." Something glittered hard and sharp in his eyes.

She made up her mind to get away, but Max appeared, no longer in skates, his expression rigid as he pulled her behind him. With blazing eyes riveted on Peterson, Max spoke to Laney.

"Is he bothering you?" he asked with a grunt.

Was he? She wasn't sure, but more than anything she didn't want Max to throw an ill-advised punch. "No. I was just telling him I don't want to be interviewed."

"I already told him that. What's the matter, Mr. Peterson? Didn't you understand me before?"

Peterson did not back up in spite of Max's tall frame and the angry set to his wide shoulders. "You should welcome the publicity, shouldn't you?" Peterson said mildly. "Laney's got no rich mother to bankroll her like Beth Morrison has. Mommy Morrison was in town just last week, you know." His gaze shifted around the arena. "What does training here cost a person, I wonder?"

Max leaned in. "None of your concern."

"No, you're right. No fun for Dad, though,

huh? Trying to pay for all this with his cab-bie business?"

He knows everything about me. Laney put her hand on Max's lower back, feeling the tense knot of muscles there. "I want to train now. Come on," she whispered.

"I'm not moving until Mr. Peterson here does," Max said. He took out his phone. "Did you need security to show you to the door or should I help you with that?"

Peterson took a step back. "No problem. I've got some more research to do anyway. I'll let you get back to your training." He cast a derisive look at Max. "Seems like you need it more than she does."

Laney put her arms around Max from be-hind, pressing her cheek to his back as she watched Peterson leave. The feel of his strong shoulders, the curve of his spine stemmed the flow of worry for a moment. He was her trainer, not her love, but she could not stop the impulse to touch him and draw comfort from the contact. She willed her breathing and his to return to normal, blinking against a sudden onslaught of tears.

He turned around in the circle of her arms and pulled her close, looking intently into her eyes. "He's got an agenda."

She nodded, chewing her lip. "I didn't want to talk about the accident."

"You don't have to. I wonder what he's after." Max smoothed her hair with his palm. "Sure you're okay?"

"What he said…about my dad." Laney bit her lip. "I know it's hard to pay for all this. The money I made in the summer waitressing hardly covered the cost of a skin suit."

He tipped her chin upward with a finger. "Your dad wants nothing else than for you to succeed, so that's what you need to do now, that's where your focus needs to be."

She pressed her face into his chest, unable to find words to tease out the worry from her gut.

"Come on, Birdie," he said. "Time to get the job done."

"Yes, sir," she said, heading for the track. Still, she cast one more look around for Hugh Peterson, but she could not find him there in the shadows.

* * *

Max guided Laney through an arduous morning of dry-land training. Her focus was off, probably not so much that anyone would notice except him. His focus was not sharp, either, though he fought valiantly against the cascade of thoughts that threatened to pull his mind from the job at hand. The day had started off with him once again humiliating himself on the ice, and he prayed Laney hadn't seen him struggling to complete one turn. Why did he persist? To push hard, then harder, expecting a different result from ruined bones that refused to heal?

You're not a competitor anymore, whiz kid. Wise up. Blaze is dead.

But something deep down, curled inside the fibers and muscles of his will, would not let it go. A futile desire existed there, hunkered down and sheltered by the anger. Why had God let everything he wanted disappear in one moment at the hands of a single careless driver? A lifetime of striving and a ridiculous level of dedication wiped out. It burned so badly sometimes he could barely stand it.

But now, with Hugh Peterson bringing up the past and someone ready to ruin Laney's skates, the anger began to broaden as he considered that Laney might lose her dream twice. His life was one thing, broken as it was. Hers was entirely another. Laney Thompson deserved only good, the best for someone who only saw the best in others.

Teeth grinding, he signaled her to continue her stair workout. He would not let anybody rob her the way they had him.

Sweat glistened on her face as she leaped up the steps sideways to work her ankles and the dozens of intricate muscles that could mean the difference between a great athletic performance and an average one. She darted a look at him when she passed. He did not return it.

Focus, Laney. Worry about winning. I'll take care of the rest. He'd decided that it was time to go on the offensive. He was going to find out exactly who Hugh Peterson was and why he was so fascinated by Laney.

Jackie joined him, and together they watched Beth hop up the steps several paces behind Laney.

"Slow," Jackie called. "Too slow."

"You try it," Beth huffed as she continued on.

Jackie shook her head.

Max shifted at the awkwardness between Beth and her coach. He felt as though he should offer support, but he was not sure how. Instead, he fired off a question. "How well do you know Beth's mother?"

Jackie started. "She pays me to coach, and I do. I don't have a close personal relationship with my employer. It's better not to."

He recognized the jibe. It was probably a fair one. He was too close to Mr. Thompson. At times, during those long sleepless nights when his aching hip kept him awake, he wondered if he had been given the trainer's job out of pity. Poor Max, who could not compete. At least he could be near the sport that was in his blood. What else was he qualified to do, anyway? Shame warmed his cheeks.

"Why do you ask?" Jackie watched as the athletes jogged down the far staircase to start again, this time leaping up to every third step. "About Beth's mother?"

"Heard she was in town a week ago, but I never saw her here. Usually parents are going to come and see how their kids are doing, you know?"

"She must have had business here. I didn't see her, either. We spoke on the phone. Mrs. Morrison is…not like other parents," Jackie said. "That's probably why we have a good working relationship."

"I'm sure she contacted Beth, anyway," Max said. By the shift in Jackie's shoulders, he knew she was anything but sure.

They went quiet, their conversation overtaken by the squeak of athletic shoes on the tile floor and the hard breathing of Beth, Laney and the two dozen men and women training to snag one of the coveted spots on the American team. Max noted with pride that Laney was first. She worked the hardest of any speed skater he'd ever met, except possibly for himself.

"Did your parents come to see you?" Jackie asked, breaking into his thoughts. "When you were training for Vancouver?"

He'd wished they hadn't, sometimes. His mother was so small, so frail and he knew when she watched him skate that she saw another child there, a tiny boy who stood on wobbly skates that dwarfed his skinny legs, trying to keep up with his older brother Max for one precious season before the seeds of disease sprouted in his bones. There had always been that lingering memory of Robby skating along with Max for every race won and nearly won. But for Max, Robby wasn't following in his memory, he was embedded in his heart, and every win was a way of carrying his brother along in this life, too.

I will win because my brother didn't.

I will thrive because You did not save him.

I will be the best, in spite of anything You can throw in my way.

But he'd failed in that quest, failed himself, failed his brother and parents.

He realized Jackie was waiting for an answer, regarding him solemnly. "Yes, my parents came to watch me." He made a pretense of checking his training schedule.

"Looks like it's time for a break," he said.

"Max," Jackie said. "Do the doctors think Laney will recover from her brain injury? Fully recover?"

"Of course," he said automatically, though he had never heard such an encouraging report from Mr. Thompson or Laney. "Why?"

Jackie pulled a set of keys from her pocket. "Her room keys. She left them behind this morning, I think."

He went for a laugh. "Hey, I've lost track of my keys plenty of times, haven't you?"

"I found them in the refrigerator."

Their eyes met. "Doesn't mean anything, Jackie."

"Maybe not," she said. "Memory is a tricky thing, and stress doesn't help."

"She remembers when it counts."

"The nightmare scared the girls."

"When?"

"Woke up screaming at the last World event, babbling about the crash." Jackie's eyes slid to him. "I guess you didn't know that."

He remained silent. He hadn't known that, hadn't heard a whisper about it. "She's going to be fine."

Jackie nodded. "I'm sure you're right. She's got what it takes deep down. If things were different, she'd be the type of girl I'd like to coach." She smiled. "I need to work for someone who can afford me, though. I didn't tell anyone where I found the keys," she murmured.

"Appreciate that," he said.

Laney passed him again on her way up the stairs, face strained with effort but continuing to work as hard as she had the first round. She was too winded to say anything, but she gave him a thumbs up.

Laney, don't let anything stop you. He shoved the keys in his pocket.

Anything.

SIX

The chatter at lunch was lively in spite of the stair workout. Max slid a plate of steamed fish in front of Laney and settled into his own chair.

"Hey," she said with a smile. "I thought Mama Love wasn't cooking fish until she could get some fresh this weekend."

Mama Love was a tiny little woman from Barbados with a giant personality who loved cooking as much as she adored the athletes, who she referred to as her dumplings.

Max winked. "I have connections. I found a new supplier who delivered some fish this morning."

Laney pinked. "You did all that because you know it's my favorite?"

He shrugged. "I'm responsible for your health and well-being, remember? You need lean protein, and fish is the best for your training regimen." He handed her a fork. "Eat."

She sampled a forkful and pronounced it delicious. Max found himself surprised again. She'd never liked the taste of capers until after her brain injury, which seemed to have rewired her taste buds along with other cognitive and perceptual areas. "Seen your dad this afternoon?"

"No. Why?"

"I wanted to ask him about Peterson. He seems like he knows the guy. Was that your impression?"

Laney drank some water. "Dad said he doesn't want to discuss it, and that's good enough for me."

"So you don't think his reaction was unusual?"

Laney shook her head. "He's been under a lot of pressure. My rehab and training costs, trying to find a new sponsor, watching me crash and the thing with my skate and the guy with the club. That's enough for a father to shoulder."

"Still…"

"Max," she snapped. "There's nothing wrong with Dad. You're just reading things into the situation, and you don't trust Peterson."

He wanted to say more, but instead he picked up his sandwich. It was not fair to press her about it. He would go to the source. "You're right. Sorry." He changed the subject. "I think you'd better eat that fish, or Mama Love will come out there and spoon feed it to you."

She did, except for a small portion she wrapped in a napkin for Cubby. Even as she chatted with Max, he noticed her gaze wandering to the door, watching for her father. It wasn't unusual for Mr. Thompson to disappear throughout the day to oversee his small fleet of drivers.

Max cleared his dishes and thanked Mama Love for cooking up the fish.

She waved a wrinkled hand. "Anything for my dumplings," she said.

"You've got more dumplings that you know what to do with," Max replied.

She laughed. "All I do is feed them."

Laney let herself into the kitchen and

wrapped the woman in a hug, kissing her cheek. "And you keep track of everyone's likes, dislikes, allergies and everything. You're amazing."

"Go on and get some rest and don't let this man work you too hard," Mama said, pinching Laney's arm. "Skin and bone. That's all that's left of her, thanks to you."

"I hope there's some muscle there, too." Laney giggled, following Max back out into the dining room and toward the hallway.

Beth caught her at the door. "Come to my room tonight," she said conspiratorially. "We're going to watch old black-and-white movies and eat junk food."

Jackie Brewster narrowed an eye in Beth's direction.

Beth blew out a breath. "Okay, no junk food, but we can still watch a movie, can't we?"

"As long as you're done by ten o'clock. You need to be suited up at seven a.m.," Jackie said.

Beth groaned. "I deserve some downtime, don't I?"

Jackie folded her arms. "You'll have all the downtime you want if you don't make the team."

Beth's eyes glittered and she opened her mouth, but instead of firing off a retort, she screwed on a sarcastic smile. "Yes, ma'am." She turned to Laney. "How about it?"

Laney shot a look at the door. "Not sure. I wanted to go over some things with my dad."

"Such a daddy's girl," Beth said, complete with eye roll, but Max thought there was a tinge of longing threaded through the sarcasm. "Suit yourself. Catch you later." She joined Tanya and Lee Ann, who were deep in conversation with several of the male athletes.

Laney's eyes once again went toward the door, but her father did not appear.

The final training session of the day was a killer. It left her body half dead with fatigue, which would be replaced by soreness once the adrenalin wore off. She helped herself to one of Mama Love's famous kitchen-sink cookies that had everything in them but nuts. Laney called her father several times without getting an answer.

She approached Max, who was intently focused on the screen of his iPad.

"Hey, Mr. Blanco," she said.

He looked up with a jerk. "Hi. What's up?"

"What are you doing on that computer, anyway? Are you cooking up another torturous training plan in there?" She edged around to see the screen, but he abruptly closed it.

"Nothing to do with training."

There was something in the way he'd hidden his work that made her wonder.

"What can I do for you?" he said.

She felt suddenly unsure. "I wondered if you'd give me a ride into town. I want to see my dad."

He checked his watch. "Kinda late. It's almost six."

"I know, but he hasn't been returning my calls and I want to ask him something." She worried her lower lip between her teeth.

"You want to ask him about what Hugh Peterson said?" Max asked gently. "About how your dad is managing to pay for everything?"

She looked away.

"Laney," he said, turning her toward him. "Your dad is an adult. He knows what he's doing. He's under stress, just like you told me earlier."

She rounded on him. "Have you been getting paid, Max?"

"Of course."

"Every month? On time?" When he tried to look away she moved closer, putting her hands on his chest, still every inch hard muscle. "I know Dad managed the National Team fees for this month, but what about your salary?"

He smiled. "Why would you ask me that, Laney? Did Peterson put these thoughts into your head?"

"No, it's because of the smoothies."

"Huh?"

"Your favorite Green Monster smoothies, the ones you buy at the Juice Shack downtown. You always said it's your favorite thing about being here at the oval. Every Wednesday, without fail, you were in town buying your smoothie."

His smile waned at the edges. "What about it?"

"You don't buy them anymore. You haven't for the past two months."

"And you assumed that's because your father hasn't been paying me, and I don't have the money?"

She nodded, watching the telltale flush steal into Max's cheeks. "Is that the reason?"

He moved away, detaching himself from her touch. "Seems like you've decided that it is. I suppose it didn't occur to you that those Green Monsters pack a lot of calories?"

"That never made you give them up before. Four years ago you used to rip through those things."

"Well, four years ago I was training for the Winter Games, Laney. In case you haven't noticed, I'm not doing that anymore. Now I'm what we used to call a 'wannabe.' I have no business partaking in energy drinks when the closest I get to training is watching you."

"That's not true, this morning…" She trailed off, realizing too late what she'd done.

He blew out a slow breath. "So you saw that, did you?"

"I'm sorry. I wasn't spying. I just got there early. You looked good…"

"Don't." He raised a palm. "Please don't do that. The one thing I cannot take from you is pity, Laney. Do me that favor, will you?"

Her throat thickened at the pain she saw in his face, how she'd intruded on a tender, raw place. She hated to make him uncomfortable, but she had to know. "Tell me if my father has been paying you."

Max stepped back, blue eyes hard. "Listen, Laney. I'm your father's employee. My private business, including my financial arrangements, is not something I'm going to talk about with you. You're the athlete, and I'm the trainer. Let's keep it that way, okay?"

He didn't wait for an answer, grabbed his clipboard and left the dining hall. She started to go after him, to smooth things over, but Beth materialized at her elbow.

"He doesn't look happy. Problems?"

"No. We're on track."

Beth toyed with the streak in her hair, the latest shade in a long line of tints. "If you need another trainer, Jackie can help you find one."

Laney stiffened. "I've got the best trainer. I'm not looking for anyone else."

She shrugged. "Just because he was great at the sport once doesn't mean he's what you need."

He is what I need. All I need. She blinked the strange thought away. "We're fine."

"I'm the big mouth who always says what's on her mind so I'm going to lay it out there. I heard your dad hired Max because he felt sorry for him."

Laney fought for breath. "That's not true."

"And because I know that you are way too soft-hearted for your own good, I'm thinking you encouraged your dad, because you felt sorry for Max, too, didn't you?" Beth's gaze bored into Laney, and she felt like an insect on a pin.

"He's an excellent trainer. If he wasn't, I wouldn't be here."

"Sure you would. Any trainer could have helped you get here, if you really have the drive. You didn't do Max a favor, you know. He's finished in speed skating, and having him hanging on to your coattails isn't going to help him find a new life for himself."

"Beth, I appreciate your interest, but I don't need your advice."

"I know, but I always give it anyway, which is why people don't like me." She put a hand on Laney's forearm. "I don't have many friends, but I consider you one of them. If you need something, a new trainer or some money to get you through, tell me."

Laney tried for a smile. "That's pretty generous from a girl who wants to knock me out of a shot at the games."

Beth went quiet for a moment. "You know as well as I do that there are plenty of girls vying for that shot. The day of the race, it doesn't matter how well you've done all season or who was the best throughout the year. It all comes down to that one race, and you have no better chance to win than I do or any of the other girls. Knocking you out wouldn't secure me a spot."

"Then why are you so willing to help me out?"

Her eyes grew soft. "You got a bum deal

because of that accident, and if I can do something for you, I will. Remember that."

Laney accepted the tight hug from her friend. "Thank you," she whispered.

"Anytime. Going to get a drink. Want one?"

Laney declined and Beth went to the kitchen to fetch a bottle of cold water. Laney noticed Tanya a few feet away, intently thumbing through a magazine, almost too intently, Laney thought.

Laney considered her options. There would be no ride into town from Max, that was certain. None of the other girls had cars on the premises. She could bike the ten miles easily, but maybe that wasn't such a great idea, all things considered.

Wandering out into the parking lot, she saw Coach Stan getting into his Mercedes.

"Hey," she said, jogging to catch him. "Can I get a ride into town?"

He started. "A bit late, isn't it?"

"I'm going to talk to my father, and then he'll bring me back. Before curfew, I promise."

After a moment of hesitation, Coach gestured her in, and she scooted into the passenger seat of the spotlessly clean car. The only thing cluttering up the vehicle was a neat plastic tub at her feet.

Coach Stan maintained the pleasant expression he always offered except for the brief moments she'd seen him fuming about some race-related difficulty. Even then it was hard to spot the signs, the clenched jaw and the pinching around the mouth that were as close as he ever got to revealing the ferocious level of competitiveness that had earned him a bronze medal in the 1976 games and followed him through decades of coaching.

He drove at a slow, steady speed, inquiring politely about her thoughts on the training regimen. Watching flakes of snow pattering down on the windshield, they lapsed into silence that grew uncomfortable. It occurred to her that Coach Stan probably knew nearly everything about her and she knew next to nothing about him except his views on speed skating strategy.

"How's your wife?" she blurted.

He started slightly. "Very well, thank you."

Stan's wife was a slender, dark-haired Asian woman whom Laney had never heard utter a dozen words at one time. "She must be excited that you're going to be the coach for the U.S. team when we go to the games."

He quirked an eyebrow and navigated around a pothole. "What makes you think I will be?"

Laney gaped. "Well, everyone thinks so. You're the best coach anywhere," she said.

He smiled, but kept his eyes fixed out the front windshield. "This is a political competition as much as an athletic one. Maybe I will be named to that position and maybe I won't."

She finally closed her mouth after trying to dislodge her foot from it. *Way to go, Laney.* "I didn't realize there was any doubt."

"You didn't know coaches have to compete for jobs, too?"

"I guess I didn't."

He sighed. "I've been coaching for thirty years and that's a lesson I've had a hard time mastering." He cleared his throat, a small, high-pitched sound. "And how is your training going? With Max?"

She flushed for some odd reason. "Fine.

Sometimes I forget you were his coach before…before the accident."

"I'll never forget," Stan said quietly. "Max would have medaled back then, for sure." She almost didn't get his last words. "But I doubt it would have made him happy."

"Why not?"

Coach Stan shifted as if he was suddenly uncomfortable on the expensive leather seats. "Max wasn't skating toward the finish line, he was skating to get away from something."

It was as if he'd spoken the thought that had been humming through her mind since she'd met Max Blanco. "What?" she breathed. "What does he need to leave behind?"

Stan blinked. "Not for me to say. Where shall I drop you, Laney?"

She gave him directions to her father's cab company and he left her at the curb. "Thank you for the ride," she said. "Where are you heading?"

He again offered the polite smile. "Out and about."

She was in such a hurry she nearly tumbled from the car, knocking his neat box of pencils and papers out the door.

"Oh, gosh," she said as she retrieved the rolling items and put them back. "It's a wonder I can even stand up on skates. Major klutz."

He said something soothing as she retrieved another item, a business card for Diane Morrison, C.E.O. of Morrison Mining. There was a handwritten number in pen underneath the silver lettering, she noticed as she slid it back into the box.

She stared at the calm profile of her coach, who did not look at her as she closed the door.

With a wave in the rearview mirror, he drove away.

SEVEN

Max went for a slow jog on the track, letting the tension roll off his shoulders. Through the windows he could see the sun mellowing toward the horizon; the temperature would be dropping rapidly. There were others running the track just then, not speed skaters, but regular folks who chatted with each other as they ran. They belonged to another world to which he could not relate. For them, the exercise was the reward, winning was not even in their vernacular.

It was the only thing in his mind. Laney would win and he would do whatever it took to make that happen.

He hated the harsh way he'd spoken to her, though he knew he had to keep things straight between them. She was the important one, the competitor, not him. Nothing could keep him from doing his job and the last thing he needed was pity from her or anyone else.

You've gone through plenty of self-pity already.

It had started out that way, as he lay in the hospital bed in the very same hospital where his brother had died. *Why me? Why my family?* But long ago that self-pity had evaporated, crystallizing into something harder, a pervasive veneer of ice that had frozen over his soul and sealed in the rage at God. What he feared most was that something would crack that crust and he would succumb to the ire that flowed silently below the surface. Once he let that rage spew forth, he knew he might never be able to stanch the flow and it would drive everyone and everything away.

After a couple of miles, the tension wound down to a bearable level and he was determined to have one more conversation with Laney before the day ended. A professional, objective chat about their goals for the morning and the notes he and Coach Stan had gone over at the lunch break. Trainer to athlete. Professional.

He headed off the track and nearly passed the kid before he noticed him sitting on a bench just outside the ice. Same skinny shoulders, same mop of red hair, maybe fourteen, maybe not, next to a pair of speed skates that were the oldest and rattiest Max had ever seen.

Max stopped. "Didn't I see you at training the other day?"

The kid jolted as if an electric current had been applied to his spine. "No."

"Sure I did."

"I left when they told me to," he said, brown eyes sparking. "You don't own the arena, anyway," he muttered.

"It wasn't an accusation," Max said after introducing himself. "What's your name?"

The boy kicked a heel into the ground, considering. "Nolan," he finally said. "You're a skating coach, aren't you?"

"Trainer."

"Used to compete?"

Max sighed. "Yes."

"I knew it. My dad took me to see the trials."

"I made the team, but I got hurt," Max heard himself saying.

Nolan's face brightened. "Yeah, yeah. You're Blaze. I watched you tons of times when you skated here."

Max felt the twin tingles of pain and pleasure that someone, anyone, remembered who he used to be. "They don't call me Blaze anymore."

Nolan shrugged. "Must have been pretty great. I mean, while it lasted."

"It was." Max sat next to him, eyeing the skates. "You want to learn how to race?"

The kid gave an offhand nod of his shaggy head. "Maybe. Classes here are dumb, though."

Dumb, Max wondered, looking at the hole in the kid's pants, or costly?

"Live close?"

"Close enough. My mom is a janitor here. Night shift. I come along sometimes. We're out on winter break now."

Max asked what grade Nolan was in.

"Eighth. Hate it. Dumb stuff we're never gonna need." He kicked his heel with renewed vigor.

"Must be one subject you like," Max said.

Nolan laughed. "Lunch. Only thing I'm good at."

"I'm thinking you're probably not too bad at gym class, either."

Nolan looked at the ground, now swinging his legs back and forth.

"Personally, I always excelled at lunch."

A grudging smile from the kid.

"You want to learn to skate?"

Nolan stopped kicking, just for a minute, giving him a quick glance. "Maybe."

Max pointed to the battered skates on the ground. "First thing is, you're gonna want to sharpen those blades."

"Yeah, I tried, but I don't know how."

Max thought quickly. "We're training on the ice tomorrow afternoon at two. Come early and I'll sharpen them for you."

Nolan's expression was hard to read. Wary? Hopeful? "What's it gonna cost?"

Somehow Max knew it must not be charity, a handout that would be more distasteful than a fee Nolan could not pay. "Information. I've got a question for you."

"About what?"

"Yesterday. Did you leave when Coach Jackie ordered you out?"

"That tough lady with the lipstick?" He looked away. "Sure."

"So you probably didn't stick around to see the race?"

"The one where that girl crashed? Man, I heard the smack all the way from the top of the bleachers. She slammed right into those pads," he chortled.

"That's what I thought." Max hid a smile. "The skater is Laney Thompson, I'm her trainer, and after the race, somebody took her skate."

"Just one? Why would anybody want do that?"

"That's what I'm trying to find out. Did you see who did it?"

"Nah. I wasn't looking that close."

"Whoever it was, they tried to get rid of it in the lake later, but that didn't work. They might have dumped it somewhere else. The woods, maybe?"

"I've spent plenty of time messing around in those woods. I can take a look, if you want. You know, in exchange for sharpening my blades."

"Deal," Max said, pumping Nolan's hand solemnly. "See you tomorrow, then."

"Hey. If I bring you something else, something I found near here, would you be interested enough to let me watch practice?"

Max figured the boy had found some old iPod or cell phone fallen from a jogger's pocket. "I'll take a look at what you've got and then we'll talk."

Something triumphant kindled in the boy's eyes. "I got something right up your alley."

"Oh, yeah? Like what?"

Nolan smiled, a cat-who-ate-the-canary grin. "Something that's gonna get my blades sharpened for life."

Max leaned forward and offered his hand to Nolan once more. "Okay, then. See you later."

Nolan didn't hesitate, shoving his cold fingers into Max's palm. "Oh, yeah. It's a deal."

A half hour later, Max was heading for the athletes' dorms. He wanted to find Laney and smooth over the awkwardness between them.

Coach Stan walked in from the direction of the parking lot.

"Have you seen Laney?" Max asked.

"Just dropped her in town at her dad's place."

Max's eyes widened. He should have known she'd find a way. He headed to the lot, fired up his pickup and pulled it onto the road, fighting the urge to speed. Laney was perfectly fine, visiting with her father, he was positive. On the way, he phoned her and she didn't answer. Then he tried Dan Thompson, who picked up on the third ring.

"Are you at the shop, Mr. Thompson?"

"No. I was…running some errands."

The man sure ran more than his share of errands. "Is Laney with you?"

"Why would she be?"

"She got a ride into town to talk to you at the shop. I tried calling her, but she didn't answer."

"Max, why do I hear worry in your voice?"

Max wrestled with telling him about his gut feeling that something was wrong. What mattered now was finding Laney.

"No reason. I'm sure she's fine, waiting

for you at the shop. Just weird that she isn't answering her phone."

"I'm on my way."

"I'll meet you there." The sun dipped below the mountains, and a dark shadow overtook his truck.

Suddenly, he did not feel quite so positive, after all.

Laney entered her father's shop, smelling the tang of engine oil and stale coffee that she had always found comforting. "Dad?" she called, poking her head into the tiny office cluttered with piles of papers, cardboard boxes and a crooked office chair that her father refused to part with.

He was not there, and neither were his two drivers, who were probably handling airport runs and downtown fares. She reached for her phone to call him and realized she'd left it on silent after she'd phoned her dad. Two missed calls from Max. She'd call him back in a minute.

She checked the even smaller kitchen. A couple of empty soda cans and plastic containers left in the sink indicated their housekeeping skills had not improved. She washed the plastic ware, gathered up the cans and headed to the garage in search of the recycling bin.

The garage was dark, the massive sliding door closed. The only vehicle parked there was an unfamiliar dark blue sports car. Moving closer, she was shocked to discover it was an Aston Martin in pristine condition. She and her father had gone to many car shows in their time, and this vehicle would have fit in with any of them with its sleek lines and immaculate interior. Where had it come from? None of her father's drivers could afford such a vehicle; neither could their employer. She heard a thump in the darkness.

"Daddy?" she whispered, skin prickling.

"Not Daddy," a voice replied. A bare overhead bulb flicked on.

Stomach twisted in fear, she watched as a short, bushy-haired man stepped into the pool of light. They stood for a moment, sizing each other up. Fear rose inside Laney's throat along with a good measure of anger. It was the man she'd seen attacking her father outside the oval.

She swallowed. "I almost didn't recognize you without your club."

He cocked his head and then smiled, giving her a full array of very white teeth. "Funny."

"Who are you?"

"Trevor Ancho," he said.

The name rippled through her memory. Hugh Peterson had asked if she knew him.

"And I already know you are the talented Laney Thompson, speed skating star." Ancho's tone was derisive. "Prone to accidents, though."

Accidents. "What did you do to my father?"

Ancho stuck his hands into the pockets of his wool coat. "What makes you think I've done anything to him?"

"Maybe because you were trying to beat him to death last time I saw you, and here you are in his place of business."

"I wasn't going to beat him to death. Bad for business. Dead people don't pay up."

She felt a trickle of dread ice up her spine. "Does he owe you money?"

He drew his hands out again, patting all his pockets and hooking his thumbs in the coat with a sigh. "Trying to give up smoking, but my hands are the enemies. Ever smoke?"

"No."

"Don't start."

She looked past Trevor to the exit, but it seemed so far away. The button to open the big garage door was on the far wall, and the thing opened so slowly she did not think she'd be able to get out before he caught her. Her phone was in her hand. Could she call Max? The police? First she had to know about her father. "What do you want?"

"To talk to your father, but now that you're here we can take care of both birds."

"Where's my dad?" she said louder.

He ignored the question. "I admire your determination and athleticism. I was an athlete myself. High school wrestling."

She waited, forcing herself to breathe slowly.

"You had that shot at the Games four years ago, but things didn't work out. Now, what you're doing here, it's not going to work out, either."

"What I'm doing? You mean trying to make the team again?"

He nodded, unwrapping a stick of gum and popping it into his mouth, offering her a stick. "Gum?"

"How do you know it's not going to work out?"

He chewed for a moment. "Lots of reasons."

"What reasons?"

"Let us just say, there are people who would like you not to compete."

Cold seeped up the concrete floor into her body. "Who doesn't want me to make the team?" she forced herself to ask. "I have a right to know."

He snapped the gum, eyes gone hard. "No, you don't have the right. You're not that important. You're just a girl trying to be important, and you're gonna have to find some other way to do that."

Her fingers found the phone and sought the emergency-dial button. "And you're going to hurt my father to make me quit?"

"No," he said. "What's between your father and me isn't your business, but if you dial the cops on that phone in your hand right now, then I'm gonna have to think about changing my mind."

She jerked her finger off the button. "Don't hurt my father. Please."

"There, you see? I knew you could be reasonable. Smart girl like you." His eyes roved her body. "Good legs, pretty face. Plenty of opportunities."

"Who wants me to quit? If I'm going to give up my dream, I should at least know a name."

His smile vanished, and he spat the gum onto the floor. "So presumptuous. That's the problem with certain women. You have no power, no rights, no leverage. You got nothing, so don't put on airs. Same thing I told your father. No rights, no power, no leverage." He stabbed a finger in the air for each point.

She flinched, legs trembling. "I want to see my dad."

"He's closer than you think." His smile was sly. "I want to show you something," he said, tone easy and calm once again. "See the car? Turn around and take a look."

She turned reluctantly.

"Nice, isn't it? That right there is a two-hundred-thousand-dollar car. Top-of-the line sound system. Carbon-ceramic brake rotors. Personalized door sills. It separates people, you know? Those who can own something like this from those who never will. You feel it when you're driving, in the pulse of the engine, the way other people look at you. They get this certain expression on their faces, which shows that they know they'll never possess a machine like this."

"It makes you feel big, doesn't it?" she muttered. "Showing off."

He was close behind her now; she smelled mint on his breath. "You're not so different. That's why you all work so hard for that piece of gold to hang around your neck, so you can show off something the rest of the world will never get a shot at."

"That's not why we do it," she whispered.

"No? And there isn't just the smallest bit of showing off in what you do? And some pride in your dad when he thinks about his baby being a champion? No vanity at all in that? Don't we all deserve a chance to see our kids do that?"

An electronic chirp indicated he had triggered the trunk release. "Take a look inside," he breathed.

Terror surged through her now, in a raging tide. She wanted to kick out at him and run for the door. But her father... She had to know.

He put a hand on the small of her back. "Go on. Look."

The small trunk was dark inside. He pushed her closer until her thighs pressed the back bumper.

Daddy. Daddy.

She prayed as she had never prayed before, entreating her Heavenly Father to not let it be what she imagined in that blackened trunk. Stiffening, she tried to resist moving closer, but now both Trevor's hands were on her back.

Her skin went ice cold. One of his hands let go for just a moment and then there was a crackling noise, a surge of fire through her limbs, which seized uncontrollably, and she could not stop herself from falling into

the trunk, arms and legs twitching. Helplessly she watched as the lid slammed closed
above her.

EIGHT

Max made it to the shop a few minutes after Dan, who stood with his hands on his hips in the kitchen.

"She's not here." Dan frowned. "Someone opened the garage door. My cabbies know to keep it closed. She called my cell several times but didn't leave a message."

Max wanted to ask why Dan hadn't answered his daughter's call, but instead he tried her phone again. No answer. "All right. Let's think it through. Where would she have gone on foot? The café? The smoothie place?" He didn't think so, but Dan jogged out the door to go check while Max paced the cement floor. His fears would be proved wrong in a moment when Laney returned, orange smoothie in hand and that big grin on her face.

The minutes ticked by. He wandered through the back office, the kitchen, thinking she might have left a note for her father. The garage offered no further clues except a discarded piece of gum and the faint smell of exhaust.

Dan returned with Officer Chen. "Hello, Mr. Blanco. Glad to see you again. I was finishing dinner at the coffee shop when Dan came in. I thought I'd see if you'd located Laney yet. Haven't come up with anything on that guy who pushed you into the pond."

Max wasn't sure if he was relieved or more concerned to have the police involved again. He was about to answer when the officer's phone rang and he stepped away to take the call. Dan stared off into space and a helpless feeling descended on Max. *Only natural to feel that way when your star athlete is AWOL.*

But he wasn't thinking about her racing skills at that moment, her potential athletic worth. He was considering, just then, her smile, her big belly laugh, the way she kept an enormous messy list on a piece of poster paper to track all the people she was praying for at any given time, the fact, he couldn't help but notice, that his name never disappeared from that list no matter how many insertions and deletions there had been.

A memory from their life before the accident surfaced: Laney, hair flying in all directions, trying to wrangle a dozen seven-and eight-year-olds on the ice, a project for foster kids she'd developed and implemented all by herself in spite of her coach's discouragement. At the time he'd agreed with them, thought it cost hours she should have been using to train, but she'd explained it to him in no uncertain terms. "Max," she'd said, thrusting a squirming boy into his hands. "You've got the same minutes in the day that I do. Make them count for something bigger than skating."

Bigger than skating? The bizarre thought had left him speechless, but after the shock wore off, he'd done his best and joined in the melee. At the end of an exhausting hour came boxes of juice and dozens of slices of pizza. The whole gaggle wound up with smiles on their faces, waving goodbye to two very exhausted elite skaters.

He'd pondered her odd pronouncement for a long while. Minutes? His life had been defined by minutes, seconds, milliseconds, but he'd only cherished those tiny increments of time when they brought him glory. It occurred to him that Laney saw the minutes of her life in an entirely different way. Skating was part of it, but not the whole. He'd never understood it, but he felt warmed nonetheless. "Is it possible she got a lift back to the dorm?" Dan mused.

"I already called Jackie. She's not there."

They both turned as Chen disconnected. "Got a call from a concerned citizen. She said she saw Laney walking on the side of the road." He paused, delicate eyebrows drawn together. "She's confused."

"What?" Dan said, gripping his arm. "Is she okay?"

"She's…unharmed. Caller reports she's somewhat incoherent."

Max's gut clenched. "Head injury? Did she fall? Where is she?"

Chen shook his head. "That's the odd thing. She's on Mountain Loop, just past the grove."

It was as if Max's body iced over from the inside out.

"But that's…" Dan started.

"The place where we got hit four years ago," Max finished.

"I'll take you," Chen said, heading for the door.

They traveled in silence, the officer driving with caution since the snow had deposited a thin cotton layer on the roadway. Max kept pressing the imaginary gas pedal under his own foot. *Faster,* he wanted to yell or wrestle Chen out of the driver's seat and take the wheel himself.

Incoherent? Laney was at the location of the horrific accident that both of them had tried so hard to put behind them?

Her room keys.

I found them in the refrigerator.

Nightmares he didn't know about.

Training drills she lost track of.

Skates she did not tie properly.

Was Laney's mind suffering the strain of trying to reclaim what she'd lost?

Don't even think it, he told himself, forcing his body into stillness as the miles passed.

Finally, they pulled onto Mountain Loop Road and the picturesque hollow of snow-mantled pines. Something in his lungs knew the place, because he found it suddenly an effort to suck in a full breath. The crunch of metal, the snapping of bones. Did Laney still hear those horrifying sounds as clearly as he did? He had eyes only for the parked pickup truck, engine running, and the woman who stood near the passenger window. She wore glasses and a knit cap that nearly covered her gray curls. She hustled up to the police car. Max and Chen got out first.

"I'm glad you're here. I was on my way to town when I saw her wandering on the side of the road, crying," the lady said. "She's been rambling about…"

Laney slammed open the truck door and launched herself at Max, tears rolling down her face, her body heaving with shuddering sobs.

"Birdie," he whispered, wrapping her tightly in his arms, willing himself to take on some of the fear he felt tingling through her limbs. *Thank God,* he heard his heart say, and for that minute it did not matter how she'd come to be on that road, or any of the circumstances that might have led her there. She was safe. It was enough. *Birdie. Birdie.*

She pressed her face so tightly to his chest he could not hear what she was saying.

"It's okay," he crooned. "Take a deep breath."

Dan hovered nearby. "What happened? How did you get here? Why?"

Officer Chen was writing notes as the gray-haired lady recounted the details. "She said," the woman offered, glancing at Laney, "she said she'd been in the trunk of a car and someone dumped her here."

Laney's head jerked up and she went rigid in Max's arms. "Yes, that's what happened. I was at Daddy's shop and Trevor Ancho was there and his Aston Martin, and he used a stun gun on me and locked me in the trunk and..."

Max tried again to get her to breathe slowly, to control the wild rush of words that he must not be deciphering properly. "Slow, Laney. Say it slow."

She breathed with him for a moment and then told them again about Trevor Ancho.

Max's mouth fell open as he listened. "Who…? Why would he do that?" he finally managed.

"He's the man who broke Dad's window. He wants me to quit racing," she said. "I thought he'd hurt Daddy. I thought Daddy was in the trunk." She began to cry again, and this time Chen guided her to the backseat of his car, insisting that she sit in the warmed interior.

Dan clutched her hand. "Laney, I'm so sorry."

Max stepped back and tried to gather his wits. The guy who'd busted into Dan's car had now locked Laney in the trunk of an Aston Martin and abducted her with the intent of pressuring her to quit racing? And he'd added the touch of dumping her at the spot of their hit-and-run?

It was bizarre.

He looked at Laney, clutching her father's hand, as Chen gave up trying to persuade her to go to the emergency room.

"Who is Trevor Ancho?" Max found himself asking Chen.

"Local businessman. Owns a fairly successful construction company."

Max caught Chen's expression and turned to Dan. "Can you think of any reason he'd do something like this?"

"No," Dan said flatly. "Can't think of one."

Laney tried to get the words to come out in a way that would make sense, but she could tell by the faces around her that her retelling was only adding confusion. When she refused again to go the hospital, Dan stepped away and let Max kneel next to her at the car door.

"Hey, Birdie," he said, giving her a smile and reaching for her hands.

She took his fingers in hers, trying not to squeeze too tightly. "Max, I'm not making it up. It happened."

He nodded, voice soothing. "We'll just get all the details ironed out, but I want you to go to the hospital, just for a check. Would you do that for me and your dad?"

A thought occurred to her, proof of her

wild claim. "Look on my back," she said, getting out of the car and pulling up her jacket.

"Laney," Max started.

"He used a stun gun or something, just below my ribs. There will be a mark."

He tried again to stop her but she yanked up the material, exposing her bare skin to the cold. "Look," she all but shrieked. "Is there a mark there?"

Dan, Chen and Max all stared at her back, as well as the lady with the gray hair. Slowly their gazes shifted to her.

"Can't you see it?"

"There's no mark, Laney," Max said quietly.

Frustration bit at her. "My jacket must have insulated my skin." She let the jacket settle back down around her middle. "But it happened. There must be tracks from his car. On the snow."

Chen shook his head. "No tracks—snow has been falling steadily for the past few hours."

Laney tried to think of some other detail she'd forgotten. She'd been locked in a trunk and abducted. There had to be some small piece of evidence to prove it. "You believe me, don't you?"

"Yes," Dan said immediately. "I do."

"What about you?" Laney said, turning her gaze to Max.

"You've been through a shock," he said.

She put her hands on his chest and made him look in her eyes. "Max, do you believe me?" She saw it there, the glimmer, the suspicion that the whole strange episode was the product of her damaged brain. The sliver of doubt lodged itself deep down inside her heart, cutting through something tender and leaving a trail of pain in its wake. Her hands fell away and she stepped back, seeing her own troubled face mirrored in his eyes.

Suddenly her limbs felt weak, every muscle and nerve; even her neck was not strong enough to hold up her chin and her head drooped. She studied the snow at her feet, the laces of her shoes, anything to avoid looking at the man who did not believe her, who thought her brain was so compromised she would create such a story.

"Laney," Max said, reaching for her.

She pulled away. "I get it. You think I made it up."

"No…" he started.

"Don't," she said, hearing an unfamiliar hardness in her own voice. "Don't pity me. Isn't that what you asked of me before?"

"I don't pity you."

"Oh, yes, Max," she said, a pent-up storm of emotion inside her begging for release. "You feel sorry for brain-damaged Laney Thompson, so addled that she's gone around the bend. The girl who needs to put up notes to remember the hot and cold water taps and can't tie her own shoelaces anymore."

"You're putting words in my mouth, Laney."

She could not stop the tide of anger and hurt that now boiled out in a bitter rush. "But truly the worst part is, you're worrying about what this means for the trials, aren't you?"

He shook his head. "That's not it at all."

"You lie," she spat, a fresh trail of tears loosing themselves down her face. "You lie, Max. Because all I am to you is an athlete, a girl with a little talent and a lot of drive who might not be able to skate fast enough to win.

I'm a commodity that you use to get close to the medal, aren't I? The means to an end."

"Laney." His voice was barely a whisper. "Please."

"It's true, Max," she said. "And why should that hurt me? You've said all along we're trainer and athlete, nothing more. Strictly professional, you and me."

Her father put a hand on her shoulder. "You're upset, baby. This isn't the time. Let's get you to the hospital."

She felt like laughing. "I think maybe it's the perfect time, Dad. Everything seems so clear right now."

So clear she thought she could hear the sound of her own heart cracking in two.

NINE

Max felt as if he was watching some strange movie as they pulled up at Trevor Ancho's place of business. He knew it wasn't police protocol to let civilians in on the questioning, but for whatever reason, Chen allowed them to follow along. The man who'd just introduced himself certainly had the same stature and build as the guy who'd bashed out Dan's truck windows, but he had never seen the face clearly. And this man, all smiles and strong handshakes, appeared completely at ease.

He heard Laney suck in a breath as she confronted him. "I told them what you did to me."

His eyebrows shot up. "Did? Do I know you?"

Laney shook off her father's arm. "You can

lie all you want, but I told them you stunned me and shoved me into the trunk of your Aston Martin and brought me to Mountain Loop Road."

Trevor blinked and shook his head. "I'm not sure which part of that I'm more surprised about, that you're accusing me of kidnapping you or the fact that you think I own an Aston Martin." He jerked a thumb behind him. "That's my one and only vehicle right there. I was just checking on one of my jobs down the mountain." He looked at Chen. "It's the grocery store remodel on Fifth." He offered an apologetic smile. "You can check with my foreman if I need an alibi. I've been chewing him out for the past few hours and he'll be happy to tell you all about it."

Officer Chen said he would check. "Mr. Ancho, am I clear in understanding that you do not own an Aston Martin?"

Ancho laughed. "Yes, sir. If I had the money for that, I wouldn't be driving a ten-year-old pickup truck, let me tell you."

"You know I'm going to run your vehicle registration information," Chen said.

"I would hope so, with these accusations

flying around. Do whatever you need to do to assure yourself I had nothing to do with hurting anybody."

Max thought the smile was a little too easy; the good-old-boy charm rang somewhat false in his ears. Or was he just looking for reasons to support Laney's story? "Laney says you are the one who broke Mr. Thompson's car window."

"Dan's? Why would I do that?"

"You know each other?" Max asked watching the flicker of emotion that passed over Dan's face. He could not decipher it quickly enough before it was gone.

"Only in passing. Used his cabs a bunch of times. Certainly got no reason to bust out his windows, do I, Dan?"

Dan went still. "No."

Officer Chen asked a few more questions and thanked Ancho politely.

"Happy to help," Ancho said. He offered a smile to Laney. "I'm sorry there's been a misunderstanding here, but I hope everything turns out well for you. You're a skater, I know from the papers. Had a string of misfortunes, haven't you? Paper said you're looking to make a comeback and I think that's just great." He frowned, looking around as though he was noticing for the first time where he happened to be. "Say, isn't Mountain Loop the place where you were hit all those years ago?"

Laney eased back a step as if she could distance herself from the memories he knew had to be assailing her at that moment.

Ancho frowned. "Weird…"

He apparently thought Laney was going to respond, but she looked at the ground instead.

With a final shrug, Ancho returned to his office.

Chen said he would be in touch with all of them and checked one last time to be sure Laney did not want medical treatment.

She shook her head and thanked the officer in a very small voice.

Max watched Dan take his daughter in his arms. He spoke low, so low Max didn't catch all of it.

"I know what kind of monster he is, Laney," Dan said.

Her head jerked up. "You know I'm telling the truth?"

"Yes, I know. And I'm going to take care of it all, don't you worry."

She gripped his arms. "You know things about him? Dad, we have to make the police see the truth."

Dan shook his head. "Listen to me. The police can't help with this."

"Why not? What's going on?" Her tone was pleading.

"I promise, I'm going to take care of it. Give me a few days."

"No, I'm scared of that man, and I don't want you doing anything crazy."

"Nothing crazy, I just need to settle something with him and this will all be over."

"Dad…"

"Trust me." He gave her a kiss on the forehead. "Trust me to fix it. You've always trusted me before and I've never betrayed that trust, have I?"

She shook her head.

He nodded. Clearing his throat he looked at Max. "All right. Drop me back in town and take this gal back to the dorms since she refuses to go to the hospital. I'll check in with you later."

Laney held on to his hand until he detached himself and all three of them squeezed into the front seat of Max's truck. It did not escape Max's notice that Laney made sure her father was in the middle. Avoiding him? He wasn't surprised.

They drove slowly, since it was now fully dark, and Max dropped Dan at his shop.

"Please be careful," Laney said, stepping out and embracing him hard before she got back in the car.

"I will." He beamed a bright smile at them both. "Go rest and hit the training hard tomorrow. I'll be there to see your ice time."

Laney didn't answer as Max waited until Dan went inside.

As they took the road back to the oval, the sound of the tires crunching in the snow was the only break in the silence.

What should he say?

I'm sorry....

I should have believed you....

You're not a commodity to me....

Nothing sounded remotely correct in his mind.

"Laney..." he finally started when he couldn't stand her silence anymore.

"Peterson mentioned Ancho's name," she blurted.

"What?"

"Hugh Peterson asked me if I knew of someone named Trevor Ancho." She glared at him. "Odd, huh?"

"Yeah." He mulled it over. "I'm going to check it out."

"No, I will."

He sighed. "Laney, I want to help you get to the bottom of this...." He read her face. "And not because it's going to impact your training or your racing or anything to do with skating. I care about you, I always have, and whatever is going on here is dangerous."

"Whatever is going on here? So now you think I was telling the truth?"

"I know you'd never make something up, Laney, it was just a lot to take in all at once." They pulled into the parking lot and he turned off the engine and reached out a hand for hers. She jerked it away.

"I'm sorry," he said.

"Don't be sorry," Laney snapped as she got out. "I'm tough. I can handle it."

"See you in the morning," he called to her back.

He heard her sniff, rubbing at her eyes with the back of her sleeve.

Though he watched until she'd safely let herself into the dorm, she did not turn around.

The door clicked close with a loud snap, leaving him alone in the night, snow settling heavily down upon him.

Laney did not cry until she was locked safely inside her room. Even then she did so quietly, her head shoved into a pillow in case the other girls might hear her sobs and come investigate. Cubby leaped softly onto the bed and curled up next to her. Laney stroked his fur, comforted by the rumbling purr.

She experienced alternating waves of fury, terror and hurt. Ancho had fooled everyone except her father. How would her father deal with a man that could lie so smoothly and cover his tracks so skillfully? And what was she supposed to do while her father "settled things" with this monster? Go on with her training?

She swallowed.

Pretend that her heart hadn't been cut in two at Max's distrust? Why did it hurt so deeply to see that doubt in his eyes? When the pain circling inside became too much to bear, she folded her hands and prayed until she ran out of words. Then she called her sister, her spirit buoyed as it always was when Jen picked up.

"Hey, sis," Laney said. "Am I interrupting your studying?"

"Please. It's a welcome distraction. I'm knee deep in human genetics. How's racing life?"

They exchanged pleasantries for a while, and Laney decided not to share with her sister the worry that weighed her down.

"I got a weird phone call today from Carol Finch," Jen said.

Carol was a long-time family friend and Realtor. "What about?"

"She heard that Dad was selling the cabin, and she was hurt that he hadn't contacted her to arrange the sale."

"What?" Laney nearly dropped the phone. The tiny cabin tucked between two mountain peaks not two hours from the oval was their refuge, the place their father went religiously every chance he got to fish, so much more than a vacation spot it was like a member of the family.

"That was my reaction, too," Jen said. "I figured it must be some kind of a mistake. Dad would never sell the cabin without telling us first." She paused. "Would he?"

"I… No. I'm sure he wouldn't. It must be a mistake, like you said."

"Yeah." Laney heard the note of indecision in her voice. "It's just that…"

Laney could fill in the blanks. "It's just that my training is ruinously expensive."

"I wasn't going to say that. It's not only you. My school isn't cheap. That's why we both work whenever we can swing it."

"But you're covering most of your tuition with scholarships. I'm the one sucking him dry."

"Laney Elise Thompson. Both Dad and Mom wanted you to have every chance to go after your dream."

"But what if it's the wrong dream, sis?" she said, voice quavering. "Maybe being a gold medalist is a selfish dream that's costing us all too much."

"Mom said God would use your skating to bring Him glory, remember? When you get that medal, you'll be able to start your skating school and give kids a better start. Isn't that what you want?"

"Yes," she said. "I'm just worried right now that the cost is too high."

"It's a higher cost when you don't do what God made you to do."

She fought against tears. "I love you, and I don't want to let you down."

"I love you, too, big sis and the only thing you could do that would disappoint me is quit." She said good-night and they made arrangements to talk again after Jen's finals were over.

Laney paced the tiny room. Had her father really decided to sell the cabin? She called his phone, but he did not answer. She longed to talk to Max, but her aching heart reminded her that Max was not what she'd thought him.

And what was that, exactly?

Her best friend?

The man she'd once been more than a little attracted to?

Old news. Old life.

She forced out a breath. *Focus on the now. What can you do to help your father?*

She could only think of one action to take. Retrieving the business card from her bag, Laney dialed the number.

"Hello," she said to the answering machine. "Mr. Peterson, this is Laney Thompson. I'm sorry we got off on the wrong foot. I'd like to meet with you as soon as possible."

Max lay perfectly still on his bed in the dorm, listening to the creaking of the floor boards as trainers and coaches tucked in for the night. Then in excruciating slow motion, the clock began to tick away the hours until morning. Though his body was tired from what seemed like an endless day, he could not fall asleep.

Why hadn't he believed Laney?

There were certainly plenty of odd goings-on lately to make him think something nefarious was afoot—the disappearing skate, the guy in the parking lot. So all that in play, and he hadn't believed she'd been forced into a trunk and left at the scene of their crash?

His disbelief was, he realized, not because of Laney. The fault lay deep within his own cowardice. Max Blanco did not want to be taken back to that place, not mentally, not physically. To believe that someone had forced Laney to that crash site purposefully meant that he, too, had been taken against his will to the darkest place, the time of deepest despair. He didn't want to return there, so he'd told himself she hadn't, either.

Coward. He'd run, sprinted, in fact, away from her claim just as fast as he'd been able.

But maybe it was better, after all. Here in the safety of complete isolation, he could allow himself to admit that he had begun to see someone else when he looked at Laney, not the athlete, not even the peer who had journeyed with him through the past arduous years. He'd started to see someone who knew him more than he wanted, who seemed to see Max Blanco as he wished he could be instead of as he actually was. The sweetness of her soul, the warmth with which she treated others, stayed in his memory. Her laughter lit his heart inside and almost illuminated the dark corners.

Almost.

He thought, then, of the bright lights of the hospital room when they had inserted the needle into his hip to harvest the bone marrow that would save his brother.

"See, Robby?" his mother murmured, tapping gentle fingers on Robby's ankles and tickling him up his legs to the tummy. "Max is going to give you his good bone juice and it's going to grow inside so you'll be healthy like him."

Robby, too sick to move, had answered with a smile, those wide eyes turned toward his older brother. And Max had believed it. His mother, his father, the chaplain, they all believed it. Max's body would heal Robby's. God had made him to save his brother.

He had thought that as the years passed, the sharp edge of pain would have dulled.

It hadn't. As agonizing as ever, it surged through him again.

Not strong enough for his brother.

No longer fast enough to win.

Not brave enough to return to the past, and without the courage to move beyond it. Stopped, like a skater with a broken blade. But Laney was not trapped. She could have a future, be a winner, but not if she looked to him for anything but training.

Good work, Blanco. You've destroyed the chance for anything more to grow.

Too weak to love her.

Too slow to be her equal.

But determined enough to help her win. That was all he had to give.

He checked the luminous dial of his watch. 3:00 a.m. Only two more hours until training time. He forced his eyes closed and went over the fitness regimen for tomorrow before he fell into a troubled sleep.

TEN

Laney immediately checked her phone the moment her eyes opened at four-thirty. No messages from her father, but one from Hugh Peterson.

"I don't know what changed your mind, but I'll take it. Can you meet me at the coffee shop in town tonight? I'll be there at six, and I'll stay until you show or they kick me out." There was a pause. "You were smart to call me. There are things you need to know."

She listened to the message twice. *Things you need to know.* Until a few days ago, she'd thought she'd known everything that mattered in her father's life and her own. Now she felt uncertain about everything. Training was usually the constant, but even that was not enough to soothe her when she recalled Ancho's not-so-subtle message. He did not want her to compete. Why? She'd not even known the man before he shoved her in his trunk.

But Dad knows Trevor Ancho. The thought burrowed into her gut and stayed there until she found herself pacing in little circles. A little worm of doubt wriggled stubbornly through her thoughts. Dan Thompson was a good man and an excellent father. She had never known her natural father and she had no desire to. He only crossed her mind once in a while, when she considered her hazel eye color and her left-handedness, which she knew did not come from Paige, her birth mother. Genetically, she was a blank, but thanks to Dan and Linda, she knew who she was in every other way.

And maybe a shred of credit had to be given to Paige, too. She'd gone through with having Jen and Laney when there were other choices to be made. On one startlingly sunny November Sunday, she'd even gone so far as taking them all to a neighborhood church, where the two girls had been delivered into a children's class. It had felt as though everyone was speaking another language where they sang the same songs and recited the presnack prayer from memory. Though Laney politely refused to participate in craft time or the story circle, unlike her sister, both of them happily wolfed down as many goldfish crackers as they could pack away, since they had not eaten since lunchtime on Saturday. It might have been an excellent start to a new life if Paige hadn't left midservice when her drug craving took over and had forgotten to pick up the children from Sunday school. Three hours, one police officer and two social workers later, the girls said goodbye to their mother and started their foray into the foster care system. Then God had brought Dan and Linda into their lives.

Their forever family. Dan had given them, given her, everything. But what had it cost him?

Forcing her mind away from the worry, Laney quickly showered, after consulting her "hot" and "cold" notes, and packed her gear.

Cubby turned up his nose at his cat food.

"I'll bring you some fish later," she said, giving him a kiss.

Opening the door she padded out into the

kitchen, startled to see Beth already there with a cup of coffee. Her face looked unusually pale, and there were dark circles under her eyes.

"You okay?" Laney said.

Beth jerked. "Oh, yeah. Couldn't sleep."

"Man trouble?" Laney joked.

"Mom trouble. Kind of the same thing."

Laney sat down next to her. "How so?"

"My mother hates my boyfriend. She's never liked any of them."

Laney had met several of Beth's boyfriends and she had to admit she didn't generally think much of them, either. "Did you break up with Cy?"

"He broke up with me." She sighed. "Said I wasn't much fun with all this training and curfews and such."

"I guess it's not easy dating a speed skater."

"Yeah. Or maybe my mother gave him a call. She's got this extensive reach that never fails to amaze me." Beth cocked her head. "I've been thinking. What about you and Max?"

"What about him?" Laney shifted. "He's my trainer. I told you."

"You two were out pretty late last night, I noticed," Beth said, tapping her fingers on the rim of her cup. "Getting to know each other better?"

"That wasn't a date," Laney said, cheeks heating up, wondering if the girls had been watching through their window as she practically bolted out of Max's truck.

"Mmm." Beth traced the top of her coffee cup with her index finger. "So you and Max are completely professional? Even though he's gorgeous and looks at you like you're the world's most perfect woman?"

Laney got up and helped herself to a bottle of water, her stomach tight. "He looks at me like I can win a gold medal. That's what I am to him. A medal contender."

"That's it?"

Remembering the look of doubt on his face, she nodded firmly. "That's it."

"So you wouldn't feel bad if he got together with someone else?" She toyed with her hair. "Say, a cute, witty, well-dressed hottie like myself?"

Laney was stunned. "You…you want to get together with Max?"

Beth shrugged. "Why not? Laney, you must have noticed the guy has the face of a model and the body to match."

Laney fiddled with the water bottle. Of course she'd noticed, but it had been other things that kept her head turned in his direction—his respect for her father, the ferocious work ethic, the way he'd spent an hour after practice one day at the Zamboni operator's house, fixing his mother's washing machine when the lady didn't have the money to hire someone. The way he cut out articles about white-water rafting and gardening for her, the times he'd researched churches in the area for her to attend and waited patiently outside while she'd done so.

Those were the things that drew her to him, that soft and tender soul that he hid so well from everyone. She realized Beth was staring at her, waiting.

"Beth, Max is my trainer, that's all. If you want to pursue a relationship with him, go ahead." She wondered if the words sounded genuine, since they'd felt like sharp glass as they passed her tongue. She began picking items from the buffet spread and tossing them into a paper bag for her midmorning snack.

Beth seemed to be saying something, but Laney was not listening until she repeated it again, more urgently.

"Not that," Beth said, taking the cellophane-wrapped cookie from Laney's fingers.

"What?"

Beth held the package up close to Laney's face. "Peanuts, see?" she said, pointing to the ingredients list. "That's why they're in the bowl labeled 'contains nuts.' Last I heard you were allergic to peanuts, aren't you?"

Laney nodded. "Thanks. I would have read the label before I ate it, though."

"Well, let's not take any chances, shall we?"

She sighed. "Yeah. Thanks again."

Coach Jackie came in. "Laney, your dorm-room door is open. Aren't you afraid the cat will escape?"

She gaped. "I left it open? Thanks." She hurried down the hallway. What if Cubby had gotten out? He could have slipped outside the building as someone entered and exited. He'd always been an indoor cat and he would never find his way back, not through the snow. She was running now.

She rounded the corner and slammed into Tanya.

"Hey, watch it," Tanya said, rubbing her arm where they'd collided. "Where's the fire?"

"Sorry," Laney called, darting around her. She made it to her room and pushed in. "Cubby?" she called. The cat was not on his cushion on the windowsill, nor under the bed. "Cubby," she shouted now, tossing cushions aside and looking under the chair.

"If you'd waited a minute I could have told you where the cat is," Tanya said from the door.

Laney jerked to her feet. "Did you see him?"

"Yeah, I walked by and he was about to escape so I put him in your bathroom and shut the door. I was going to tell you if you'd have slowed down long enough."

Laney wrenched open the bathroom door. Cubby sat serenely on the tile floor, washing his whiskers with a delicate paw.

She scooped him up and kissed him between the ears, returning to the outer room. "Tanya, thank you for shutting him in there. I don't know what I'd do if I lost him."

Tanya shrugged. "No biggie. I used to have a beagle named Pedro that was a complete escape artist, so I'm good at pet wrangling." After a slow look around the room, her eyes landed on Laney's prayer poster. "What's that for?"

"People I'm praying for. I used to be able to remember the list, but since the accident I've got to write everything down."

A frown crept across her face. "Why am I up there?"

"You said your grandma had a stroke."

Tanya's eyes widened. "And you remembered that?"

Laney nodded. "Sure."

"Why?"

"Because we're a family here and we're supposed to take care of each other."

Tanya shifted and looked away. "I'm not sure everyone sees it that way, Laney."

"Well, I do. How is your grandma, anyway?"

"Much better. She went back to her house

and that helped her more than anything. She just wants to putter around in her vegetable garden and she's happy. That's why she lives in California, so she can plant all year round. I'm going to visit her after the trials if I can come up with the cash." She laughed. "It's her goal before she passes to teach me how to cook, and so far all I've mastered is the art of the grilled-cheese sandwich."

"I'm so glad she's better."

"Me, too." Tanya turned to leave. "But maybe you can leave my name up there, anyway."

Laney gave her a smile. "Of course. Anything in particular I should pray about?"

Tanya heaved a deep sigh. "Just everything," she said as she left.

Laney gave Cubby a good scratch behind the ears and made sure his cushion was in the perfect spot on the window sill to catch the afternoon sun. As she let herself out and carefully closed the door, she wondered how she could have been so careless before.

Or maybe someone else had opened it? *Don't get paranoid, Laney.* Trevor Ancho was out to get her, but he didn't have access to the athlete dorms. Nevertheless, she made sure this time the door was definitely locked.

Max didn't bother to ask Laney if she'd eaten breakfast, and she didn't offer her cheerful morning hello. As a matter of fact, she avoided eye contact altogether, enlisting Tanya to assist her with the series of turn-belt exercises, the arduous process of wrapping a long nylon belt around two people, then, as one held steady, the other used resistance to lean hard and simulate the moves they would replicate on the ice. It wasn't Laney's favorite, he knew. They headed directly into a round of weight lifting, stationary biking and exercise-ball routines. He led her through the activities without extra comment. She worked hard, she always did, but her pacing was off, and he had to wait for her to refocus several times when she kept sneaking peeks at the door.

They were both relieved to see Dan show up at the gym.

Laney wrapped him in a hug, such joy palpable on her face that it made Max's heart speed up a fraction.

"Where have you been?" she asked.

"Had some paperwork to do." Her dad squeezed her. "How's the training going?"

Max shrugged. "Slow start."

Dan gripped her shoulders. "Listen, kiddo. You're here to make the team. That's your only job. Don't forget it, okay?"

Officer Chen entered and caught the attention of every athlete in the place. He smiled cordially at Coach Stan, who approached him immediately.

"I'm here to talk to Laney Thompson," he said.

"What is the problem?" Stan asked.

Chen offered him a thoughtful look. "I'll leave it up to Ms. Thompson to fill you in. May I talk to her for a moment?"

Coach Stan agreed and stepped back to allow them some privacy.

Max didn't consider extending the same courtesy. If there was something to be learned about the current situation, he wasn't about to be shuttled aside.

Chen greeted Laney, Max and Dan. "I'm just reporting back."

"Did you find anything to prove he did what I said?" Laney demanded.

"Actually—" Chen shook his head "—no. Mr. Ancho's foreman corroborated his story that he was at a job site for several hours before we got the call about you."

"His foreman is lying," Laney said. "To keep his job."

Chen continued. "And Mr. Ancho does not own an Aston Martin, according to the DMV records."

Laney bent as if bowing under a crushing weight. "I can't believe he's going to get away with it."

"Still investigating," Chen said. "Filling you in on what I've got so far."

They thanked him and he left, promising to call again soon.

It did not take long for Stan and Jackie to join them, faces troubled.

"Look," Stan said, over the whirring of stationary bikes and the clang of free weights, "I appreciate your right to privacy, but I need to know what's going on."

Laney shot him a worried look. "It's nothing. Everything is fine."

"When you have a police officer coming to visit," Stan said quietly, "that kind of thing draws attention. Since the missing-skate problem, that makes two visits from law enforcement since you arrived."

"It's not her fault," Max said. "She hasn't done anything wrong."

"It doesn't matter about fault," Jackie said. "It matters about propriety. We can't have the trials painted by scandal. We've had that before and it's not fair to these athletes who have given their lives to the sport. You need to make it clear what happened."

"It doesn't affect anyone but me," Laney said.

Though Max had never seen Coach Stan angry before, the man's face darkened. "Look around, Laney," he said quietly. "Every single athlete in here has an eye on you, wondering what's going on. You are affecting each one of these kids. I need to know the truth."

Laney's face flushed scarlet as she quietly told them about the incident with Trevor

Ancho. Both coaches stared at her when she stumbled to a halt.

Coach Stan cleared his throat. "So you accused this Ancho of locking you in a trunk of a car that the police say he doesn't own?"

Max edged closer. "She didn't make it up."

He blinked. "I didn't say she did."

"She was…confused, perhaps?" Jackie offered.

"No," Laney said. "It wasn't because of the brain injury, so please don't imply that."

"We're going to get it all straightened out," Dan said, tucking Laney under his arm. She continued to look at the floor.

Coach Stan lowered his voice to just above a whisper. "I'm going to strongly advise you three to do nothing of the sort. Let the matter drop and focus on your training. That's the only choice you've got here."

Max straightened. "Do I hear a threat coming?"

Coach Stan met his gaze. "You know how the game is played. If there's a situation that will impact the sport negatively or embarrass the speed skating committee in any way, they will insist on withdrawal."

"You wouldn't do that, Stan," Max murmured. "I know you, and you wouldn't do that."

"It's her last chance to stand on that podium," Dan said, arm still firmly around his daughter.

"I've been at this coaching thing a long time, so I'm getting to the end of my career. It's my final shot at possibly coaching a team at the Games, so I understand about last chances." Stan's face looked suddenly haggard. "I've got to look at what's fair for all of the kids training, and for some of them it's their last shot at it, too." He took Laney's hand. "Do what you're here for, Laney, and don't give me, or the committee, a reason to take action."

She nodded without meeting his eye, and he walked away.

Jackie pursed her lips and blew out a sigh. "You've got what it takes to win. If someone else beats you, then that's the way it goes, but don't defeat yourself."

She headed back to the weights and barked out orders to Beth, who was making a half-hearted effort.

Max took Laney's hand, though she tried to snatch it away. "Step outside with me."

"I don't want…"

"I didn't ask if you wanted to." He pulled her out of the weight room into an empty break area with a round table and a vending machine.

"Why did you stand up for me?" she yelled at him when they'd crossed the threshold. "You don't believe me."

"Yes," he said after a breath, "I do. I thought about it for a long time last night and if you say Trevor Ancho shoved you into the trunk, then I believe you."

She crossed her arms. "Why not before?"

Why not before? That realization hadn't sunk in until he stood under the morning shower while the water ran cold. "I didn't want to think that someone was trying to take away your dream again. It was easier not to believe it."

She frowned. "We both still have a lot of hurt about what happened."

He huffed out a breath, thinking he would try for something witty, soothing. It didn't work. "I...I haven't healed well...inside, I mean."

The anger fell away and she stood there with that gentle quirk to her lips and the compassion in her eyes that nearly broke his heart.

"I know it's hard," she said "I figured it must be too much sometimes, being around me and all this. You're angry still."

"Uh-huh, and I didn't realize how angry until we were there again, you and me, at that exact spot where I lost myself. I didn't ever want to go back there. Ever."

"Max, what are you afraid of?"

Afraid of. The words circled in his consciousness. He hadn't thought he was afraid anymore of anything, that he had nothing left to lose that mattered. Because he'd already lost his brother. His racing. And her. "I think that if I have to revisit the past, something might..." He looked away.

Laney came close and put her hand on his shoulder. "Something might what?" Her voice was soft. "Tell me, Max."

He wanted to pull away from her fingers, which had now moved up to his cheek. Instead, he pressed her palm there, reminding himself that she was real, she had survived and thrived, willing the joy and optimism and happiness she experienced to somehow embed itself in him. Then her arms were around his neck, mouth inches from his as she whispered. "You're afraid it's all still there, aren't you? All that anger and hurt and loss, but it's deeper than losing your racing, isn't it? What are you afraid to look back and see?"

From somewhere deep inside it welled up, a darker fear than he had ever been able to put into words.

I am afraid I will look back and find there is no one there and I am alone.

He brushed his lips to her forehead, the warm satiny spot that made his heart pound. He wanted to tell her then, about his grief, and failures that couldn't be weathered no matter how strong the body, how brave the spirit.

How indifferent the God.

Instead, he allowed himself to feel the softness of her frame pressed to his, and let the comfort of her touch push away the shadows.

ELEVEN

Laney realized that Coach Stan was right. Max did not race toward something, but away from it. "Max, whatever it is, God can bring you past it."

He stiffened and tried to step away. "Let's not do this."

But she gripped the fabric of his jacket. "He's the only way, and He can give you peace. Nothing in this world and no one else can do that."

"Laney, you're wrong. God left me in this place. His choice. He could have saved Robby."

"Robby? Your little brother?" Laney said, not allowing him to look away. "He died young, you said, of leukemia." The pieces fell together and she let out a breath.

The little muscles in his jaw twitched. "If

God didn't want to raise His mighty hand to save a kid, then He could have at least let me do it. Would that have upset the balance of the universe?" Bitterness coursed through his words. "I should have saved him. We were a perfect match."

"But how could you have…" Her eyes widened. "You gave him your bone marrow?"

He took her hands and moved her away. "Laney, we are not going to talk about this."

She clasped his forearms. "Yes, we are. We need to. You need to."

A clearing of the throat startled them both. Beth stood, eyebrow raised, hand on one hip.

"I suppose this is some training technique to undo the mess you just made of things by bringing the cops here?" Beth demanded.

"I didn't bring them here," Laney said, letting go of Max.

"Yeah? Well, all the kids are wondering what you did, Laney. Rumors are breaking speed records in there. Are you going to enlighten us?"

"No," Max said. "She's not going to explain anything, and there's nothing to talk about but the workout that you're both shirking right now."

Beth's eyes glittered. "Boy, Laney. I wish I had a trainer like yours. So dedicated, no matter what's stacked against you." She tucked her hair behind her ears. "You know Max, we never see you at the after-hours stuff. Isn't team bonding important? I'm hosting a dominoes tournament tonight. Come."

It sounded like a demand. Laney wanted to tug Max away from Beth's admiring gaze. She didn't need to.

He headed for the door. "I've got a lot of work to catch up on, Beth, but thanks anyway."

Beth offered up a pout. "Working on a press release so Laney will have something to say about her life of crime?"

Laney's mouth fell open.

"I really should drop by more often," came a voice from the doorway. "I thought you all just talked about skating and winning gold medals."

Beth's face blanched as she took in the

heavyset woman with long silvered hair that fell in unkempt waves around her face.

"Mom. What are you doing here?"

The woman extended a hand to Max. "Diane Morrison. I don't think we've officially met."

"A pleasure," Max said.

Laney had only seen Beth's mother in online pictures and newspaper articles, dressed in smart blazers and pant suits. In her current outfit of jeans and a puffy down vest, no one would guess she was a powerful businesswoman.

Her eyes traveled to Laney. "Hello, Laney. What's this I hear about you getting locked up in trunks?"

Laney's fact went hot. News, especially bizarre news, really did travel fast. "I…"

Diane waved a hand and laughed. "Don't worry, sweetie. I'm in the public eye enough to know that half the things you hear are more fiction than fact. Anyway, I'm not here to interrogate. I've got a meeting that's going to keep me away from the trials, so I thought I'd do the mommy thing and check in on my daughter while I had the chance." She offered

Beth a smile. "Coach Jackie said you're behaving. I suspect she, too, may be giving me fiction along with the fact, but I'm happy to see you."

Beth rolled her eyes. "I'm training, that's all. That's what I'm supposed to be doing, isn't it?"

"Good, that leaves you no extra time for getting into trouble." Diane's words were light, but there was a steely tone hidden underneath. "Let's go have a chat. See you all on the ice later."

With Diane's arm draped around Beth's stiff shoulders, the two left the room.

"How did she hear about it all so quickly?" Laney mused.

"Doesn't matter," Max said, steering her to the door. "You've got a workout to finish. Ice time at two."

She mentally calculated. Ice time went for roughly three hours, counting cooldown and coach's notes. Then she'd need to find another ride to town to meet Hugh Peterson. Max was staring at her with a raised eyebrow.

"What are you planning?"

"Planning?"

"Yep, you're thinking about something and it isn't racing strategy. Don't bother to make up a story. You're not a convincing fibber."

It would be better to keep him out of it. Max was already in the awkward position of having to defend his athlete from the wildfire spread of rumor. She knew she was risking her spot on the team, and Max's job, too, by going to see Hugh Peterson. Tell him? Or not? He was her trainer, nothing more, she told herself severely, even as the memory of his lips on her skin tingled every nerve.

Tell him? But he would neither understand nor approve of anything that wasn't moving her toward the Winter Games. "I can't just pretend nothing has happened."

"Not pretend, just leave it on the bench. You have a job to do."

She tried to edge around him. "Let's go before they wonder what happened to us."

"Laney," he said, putting his hands on her shoulders.

Her breathing hitched. When God had made those eyes, she thought, he must have mixed in just a little bit of the sky, the windswept, California sky where the ocean met the air. She readied herself for a directive. Instead, he offered a request.

"Do something for me." He leaned close. "Please do not leave this training facility for any reason unless I'm with you."

She tried to wriggle away but he held her fast. "I'm not a prisoner here, am I?"

"Not a prisoner, but much too important to risk anything happening." He put a finger to her lips when she started to respond. "Not because of the skating, Laney."

"Why, then?" she whispered.

"Because…" He blew out a breath. "Just do what I'm asking. Will you?"

Why did his fingers awaken trails of longing in her soul? How would she lie to him and sneak out to meet Hugh Peterson? His blue gaze seemed to wash away all her pretenses and set her feelings tumbling on capricious waves.

"I'm not going to lie to you, Max," she breathed.

"And I appreciate that."

"So I'm not going to answer at all." Before

he could respond, she broke away and sprinted for the weight room.

Max figured the best way to be both Laney's trainer and her friend was to watch her like the proverbial hawk, which he did through the remainder of her workout. During lunch, he managed to stay in the dining hall, ears straining to hear the sound of her door opening at the other end of the hallway. He didn't know what she had planned, but he knew something was brewing in that maddeningly lovely head of hers, some plan to help her father out of whatever situation he'd become ensnared in.

Beth had not eaten with them, and he figured she was off with her mother. He was uncomfortable with the flirty tone he'd heard in her voice. Jackie sat alone, writing meticulous training notes on a yellow pad.

"A coach's work is never done," he said.

She started, as if she hadn't known he was there. "Yes, that's true." She took off her glasses and rubbed her eyes. "Where's Dan?"

"Didn't make it here for lunch. Must have had some things to attend to."

Jackie drummed her manicured fingers on the tabletop. "You know, if you combined Dan's zeal for the sport with Diane's funds you'd have the perfect speed skating parent."

"Yeah, I guess you're right." He thought about his own parents, who'd provided everything he'd needed to make his dreams come true, but neither one had ever really had a passion for the sport, not the kind of interest Dan Thompson had for speed skating. "Diane doesn't get it?"

"Oh, she's competitive, but it doesn't matter if it's skating, sailing or selling." She shook her head. "I'm being indiscreet. She tries her best."

"It's not easy parenting, or so I gather."

"No."

"Does your son skate?"

"My son?" She sighed. "Yes."

"With your tutelage, he must be pretty good."

"He could have been." Her eyes wandered to the falling snow outside. "But he felt my passion for the sport was bigger than my passion for him. I guess that's why I pity Dan.

He loves skating and he loves Laney, but that's not enough."

"Why?"

"Because winning gold takes more than love, Max. And Dan has gotten himself in too deep."

The trickle of dread turned into a flood. "Too deep into what, Jackie?"

She turned tired eyes on him. "Just train her. That's all you can do."

He watched her leave, but the worry stayed lodged inside his gut. Dan Thompson was in trouble, but what action could he take? The giant clock above the sideboard ticked away the moments with ruthless persistence.

Nearly two o'clock. Ice time.

He insisted that Laney go with him to the arena, relieved when she did not resist. While she suited up, his eyes roved the echoing space. No sign of Nolan. Maybe his mother was off shift and he couldn't get a ride. Perhaps he should have given the kid a phone number or something.

"Hey," Nolan said, emerging from a seat in the shadows.

"Thought you weren't coming."

"Deal's a deal." Nolan handed the skates to Max, who turned them over and fastened them tightly into a metal jig that secured them in place.

"It's going to take me a while," Max said, applying honing oil to the sharpening stone and gliding it gently over the blade. "You're going to fly when you try these out."

"So that's how you do it," Nolan said, crouching next to Max. "I couldn't figure it out."

"Did you have a chance to scope out the woods?"

Nolan nodded. "Didn't find a blade, but I brought you that other something I found. I figured I could give it to you in exchange for free sharpening and stuff." Nolan handed over a nylon bag, which he unzipped. There was a hard case inside, and Nolan opened the catches. "What do you think of this?"

Max studied the contents, the rough rectangular sharpening stones along with one made of marble and a bottle of oil stowed neatly in their respective spaces. "Where did you get it?"

Nolan's smile wavered. "I found it."

"Where?"

"In the backseat of a car parked in a junk-yard just outside of town."

"Recently?"

"Close to four years ago." Nolan folded his arms. "I was still in elementary school. After my dad took off, my mom worked all the time so I could go wherever I wanted in the afternoons. Junkyard was cool and most of the time nobody was there."

"And you took it from the backseat of a car?"

"Hey, I didn't steal it, if that's what you're thinking. Car was gonna be junked."

Max realized his expression must be formidable so he went for a smile. "I know you didn't steal it. This is a professional sharpening kit. It's expensive. Can't imagine what it was doing a junkyard, is all."

"Me, neither. And look at this." Nolan pulled up the foam liner that housed the stones and removed a picture of a group of people in speed skating gear, arms linked, grinning for the camera. "That girl there. She's the one who crashed into the pads, right?"

"Yes," he murmured. "That's Laney Thompson." Her smile was luminous, eyes sparkling with mischief, as she hugged her companions close. On one side, Tanya Crowley, on the other, Beth Morrison, Jackie Brewster and a young man he'd raced and beaten regularly in his past life whose name he couldn't remember. "It was taken just before the last qualifiers." It hurt to say the words, to see the happiness and promise etched on those young faces as he knew it had been on his own.

Max's mind whirled. "You found this in a junkyard car. Anything else there with the kit? Or in the junkyard?"

"Nah." Nolan shrugged. "Bunch of old rusted parts and this one nicer car. I wondered why they were going to scrap it. Only dented a little and the front windshield cracked."

Front windshield cracked. Max swallowed. "Do you remember what type of car it was?"

"White. Four doors. That's all I remember."

"Do you suppose," Max said, forcing his

voice to stay in the quiet range, "that the car is still there?"

"Dunno. Haven't been there much since. Probably crushed it, so I'm glad I got the kit out before they did that."

A rush of disappointment nearly left Max breathless. He focused on finishing the sharpening. "Tell you what. Leave that here with me and I promise I'll sharpen your skates anytime you need it done."

Nolan shrugged. "Okay, I guess, but what happens when you all leave town?"

"Then I'll get you another sharpening kit." Max handed him the skates. "Put them on and let's see how fast you can go."

While the boy bent to lace on the skates, Max carefully repacked the photo into the kit and stowed it in his duffel bag, zipping it tightly closed. "One more thing, Nolan. Can you show me where this junkyard is?"

Nolan put the guards on his skates and made a beeline for the ice. "Sure. I can be here tomorrow morning if you want."

"That's good," Max said.

"Are you gonna keep the picture, too?" Nolan asked.

"I think so," Max said, though he didn't need the photo to remember the details. After all, he was the one who'd taken it.

TWELVE

Laney threw herself into ice time with as much vigor as she could muster. The fast laps were just what she needed. Bunched in with the other skaters, the ice dampened with buckets of water to make the surface less brittle and primed for speed, there was no room left over for preoccupation.

Laney relished the opportunity to focus her mind on one thing and one thing only: going fast and hard over ice, the thing she loved more than any other activity on earth. It was not a racing situation, so she felt no pressure, and even the fatigue held off until nearly the end of the exercises. Then, as they circled around to hear Coach Stan's comments, Laney noticed the blank expression on Max's face.

Of all the people to lose focus. She waited

until they broke to go and tease him. "Day-dreaming?"

He did not smile.

"What's wrong?"

He held up her cell phone. "You got a text while you were skating."

She flushed. "You shouldn't be checking my texts."

"Didn't have to. You didn't have your phone locked and the text popped up." He thrust it at her. "You've arranged a meeting with Hugh Peterson."

She raised her chin. "Yes, I have."

"That's a bad idea."

"He knows something. He mentioned Ancho's name, and besides…"

"Besides what?"

"I think my father needs the money."

Max started to answer and then looked away toward the great domed ceiling of the arena.

"You think so, too, don't you?" she said quietly.

"Not my place."

"I'm being really careful. We're meeting at a coffee shop, a public spot, at the not-soscary hour of six o'clock. No bogeymen out at that time."

He still didn't smile. She tried to change the subject. "Saw you sharpening that boy's skates. You're going to ruin your grizzly-bear reputation."

"His name is Nolan, and you're not going to believe what he gave me."

"What?"

"Go get out of your skin suit and I'll tell you on the way to town. We don't want to be late for Mr. Peterson."

She opened her mouth, then closed it. When Max was determined, something dangerous flashed down in the depths of his eyes, turning them flat and cold. She'd seen it just before races when he'd broken world records and crushed his competitors. It was there now, just as dangerous.

In a few minutes she was back in sweats, gear safely stowed, and sitting in the passenger seat of Max's truck. He handed her a photo.

Emotions rushed to the surface as she peered at it. "I remember this. It was just before…" She swallowed. "Well, anyway, where did you get it?"

He directed her to open the duffel bag near her feet and she examined the sharpening kit while he retold Nolan's story.

She made him tell it again. "What you're saying is that you think Nolan found the car that hit us?"

"It's a possibility," he said. "Small white car, cracked windshield, with speed skating equipment inside and a photo taken before the accident. That's pretty coincidental."

"And that car isn't there anymore."

"Probably not, but there might be some of it left."

She shook her head to clear it and suddenly there were tears. Everything inside went all wobbly.

Max grabbed her hand. "I'm sorry to bring it all up again."

"I don't want to remember it," she whispered. "I think that's why I never have. I don't want to remember, like you. I've moved on. In the past few years I've gotten flashes of memory, but I turn it off because I want it to stay buried."

He gripped her fingers, his skin warm, hers cold.

"I'm sorry, Laney. I don't want to go back there, either, but I think whatever happened then is connected to what's going on now."

She sniffed. "How could it be, Max? How could that terrible accident have the slightest thing to do with my skating? Or Trevor Ancho? That was years ago."

"I don't have those answers yet, but the junkyard is a place to start."

"So you're going to check it out? On your own? Without the police?"

He ran a hand through his hair, which pushed it more into a rumpled state than it had been. She longed to finger the black wave that fell across his eyebrow.

"I think we need to be careful not to draw any more attention to you right now, and going to the cops with Nolan's story isn't going to help much. Let me check it out. If there's anything to find, I'll go to the cops without involving you."

She gripped his palm. "No, Max. I'm in it. I'm going with you to check out the junkyard."

He withdrew his hands. "It's better if you don't."

She fished a tissue from her jacket pocket and wiped her face, then collected her flyaway hair into a more presentable shape. Plastering a smile on her face, she took a calming breath. "Well, you butted in on my visit with Peterson, so consider me your partner from here on in."

The winter sun was low on the horizon, casting shifting shadows over the snow-clad ground. His face was dead serious. "Laney, you could lose your spot for the trials."

"We'll be careful."

He banged his palms on the steering wheel. "If you miss out on the team again, because of choices I made, I won't be able to forgive myself."

She joined his hand once more with her own and grazed her lips over his knuckles before planting a soft kiss on his thumb. "I think that's your whole problem, Mr.

Blanco. You haven't forgiven yourself for a lot of things."

Max didn't answer, but she saw him swallow convulsively and he allowed his hand to rest in hers until he pulled into a space in front of a wood-sided coffee shop. A sign with cheerful red trim proclaimed it The Daily Grind. Cutting the engine, he shook his head. "How about we take it one step at a time? Let's find out what the good Mr. Peterson has to say."

"Is this like the 'you've gotta put on the skates before you can start to sprint' advice you usually give me?" she said with a grin.

The look he gave her seemed exasperated and tender. "Birdie, you are something else."

She got out of the truck, savoring the nickname, letting it roll around her heart just for a moment, reminding her of the sweet bond they used to have, the time captured for one split second in the photo. Though he didn't know it, she remembered him taking the picture, his strong shoulders silhouetted in his skin suit, smile radiating confidence and something more, admiration for her. Love, even?

Doesn't matter what it was, she reminded herself sternly. *He's your trainer only, and he's made it abundantly clear that's all he wants to be.* Something in her heart thrilled anyway, as she walked close to him, a part of her that did not seem to hear anything but the rush of warmth she felt as he put a hand on the small of her back and led her inside.

Max held the door for her and they entered the small shop, the air redolent with coffee, wooden tables filled with customers sipping lattes, chatting and peering at their laptops. He tried not to look too obvious as he scanned the tables for Hugh Peterson. Finally Max spotted him at the very back of the shop, in a small battered booth festooned with pictures of Frank Sinatra in the early years. As they wove their way through the scattered clusters of people, Max was startled to spot Jackie, Tanya and Beth sitting at a corner table. He fixed on a smile and went to greet them, Laney following.

"Hello there," he said.

"Hey, girls," Laney said brightly. "Had a caffeine craving?"

Beth raised her cup in salute. "Decaf latte with cream. Even the prisoners get treats once in a while."

Jackie did not rise to the bait. Instead, she sipped her black coffee.

Tanya laughed. "I'm just tagging along, soaking up the strategy talk."

Jackie caught Max's distracted look. "Meeting someone?" she said.

He was not sure how to respond, how much to make public. Trevor Ancho appeared to be the enemy, but he had a feeling Ancho wasn't the only one interested in seeing Laney fail.

Laney saved him from replying. "Just gonna talk to the reporter. See if I can set up an interview quick in case I crash into another wall and have to retire or something."

"You won't crash," Tanya said. "I'll bet you got it all out of your system."

Beth sipped her drink through a straw. "Never know, Tanya. Any of us can go down at any time and take their fellow skaters right along with them." She was not smiling when she said it, until she looked at Max. At him, she beamed a breathtaking grin.

Jackie's face was grave as she studied Beth.

"Well," she said finally. "We don't want to make you late for your meeting."

Feeling the three women staring at them, Max led Laney through the crowd and slid into the booth across from Hugh, Laney beside him.

Hugh chewed on his mustache, sat back with folded arms. "Ms. Thompson, I didn't think you were going to bring your bodyguard with you."

"Max isn't a bodyguard," Laney said.

Unless I need to be. "You wanted to talk to Laney, so talk. And we've got some questions of our own to ask."

Hugh sucked down a mouthful of coffee from a chipped brown mug. "What might those be?"

"What do you know about Trevor Ancho?"

Hugh swallowed and wiped his mustache with the back of his hand. "I know he's the reason I can't see out of my left eye and why every time it rains my shoulder gives me fits."

Max wanted to wait, to let the silence lengthen until Hugh felt the need to fill it.

Unfortunately, he hadn't clued Laney in on the plan.

"What are you talking about?" she said.

"I mean, I was the journalist who was assigned to your hit-and-run. I got there while you two were being loaded up in the ambulance. You," he pointed at Laney, "were mumbling about a white car with a cracked windshield."

Laney blanched, and Max scooted closer to put an arm around her.

"It was snowing pretty hard by then, and the cops were photographing, so I did a little exploring on my own, saw some tire tracks leading up the mountain, but I lost them after a while. Hit-and-run. Somebody driving drunk who didn't want to face the music. End of story, or so I thought."

Max felt her tremble. His own stomach was in knots. Someone who didn't want to face the music left two people to die in the snow. He cleared his throat. "Go on."

"Two days later I'm in a bar in Levinston, that's a town about ten miles from here, and there's a guy there, who'd had way too much to drink. He starts talking about this job he did, getting rid of a car, a white car that he was ordered to crush. Couldn't figure why someone would want to ruin a perfectly good car with only a small dent in the fender and a cracked windshield."

Laney moaned. "I feel sick."

Max asked the waitress for a glass of water and insisted Laney drink some. "Did you confront the guy?"

"I arranged to meet with him, for a small fee, of course, at a park in Levinston, only someone else got wind of the meeting and two guys were waiting for us. Beat us both within an inch of our lives. Guy from the bar managed to get away and I never saw him again. Me, they left for dead, but I was stubborn enough to live and here I am. Took me a long time to get my health back, years in fact. Had to move around for a while to make ends meet, but now I'm back, ready to see things made right."

"What does Trevor Ancho have to do with all this?"

"The guy from the bar dropped his wallet, and I found Trevor Ancho's name on a piece of paper."

"Doesn't prove anything."

"No, it doesn't. Ancho's a contractor here, well respected and upstanding citizen, but I happen to know he dabbles in the loan-shark business and he's dirty." Peterson put down his coffee mug. "I think he had something to do with making that car disappear. I don't know why and I don't know how, but if he is responsible and paid those guys to beat me up to get me off the trail, he's going down. If it takes the rest of my life, I'll see to it."

Max tried to read him. "So this is a revenge thing for you? To bring Ancho down?"

Peterson gave him a hard smile. "I don't expect you to understand this, son, because you never spent time in the Hanoi Hilton like I did during the Vietnam War. You were never tortured and dehumanized like I was. It changes you. For me, it left me knowing that I would never allow a human being to brutalize me again. Ancho did, and he's going to pay for that."

Peterson's face was a hard mask with a strong current running underneath.

"Why Laney, then?" Max asked. "Why have you been trying so hard to talk to her?"

"Because you saw the driver of that white car," Peterson said, eyes riveted on her. "You are the only one who witnessed it, and I've heard you're beginning to have some memory return."

"Who did you hear that from?"

He shrugged. "You hang around the arena long enough, you hear things. My dad was Canadian, and we're big speed skating fans. I like to watch as many races and training sessions as I can." His eyes narrowed. "Until they kick me out."

A tiny beep from Hugh's phone drew his attention. "I've got to go. I have an appointment." He leaned close. "If I'm right, and Trevor Ancho was responsible for helping that hit-and-run driver escape, then he's not going to want you to remember that accident because whatever you have buried in that memory of yours can put him away."

"The police..." Laney started.

"Aren't going to do a thing unless I come up with some compelling proof, and so far I've got nothing concrete. They did their investigation looking for that white car, and it's not a priority for them anymore."

"I think there's something else," Max said. "There's some other connection that you're not telling us. Ancho's pretty bold if he's behind messing with Laney's skate and forcing her into the trunk of his car."

Hugh's eyebrows shot up as Max recounted the abduction attempt. "Man," Peterson muttered. "Ancho really is getting desperate." He flashed a wolfish grin. "Excellent."

"You hinted before that my dad was involved. How?" Laney said.

Hugh blinked. "Listen, kid. It's not easy being a dad. I know. I've tried and failed. Dan doesn't want to talk to me, and I get that. He did what he had to do. Unfortunately, he didn't realize who he was dealing with."

"What does that mean?" Laney snapped. "Please stop talking in riddles."

"All right, facts only. But later. I have to go, I'll be in touch." He slid over a card.

Max read *Sports World Magazine* in tiny gold letters.

"I do write for a sports magazine. Check it out." He fixed Laney with a look. "And I really will pay for an interview, because when

I get to the bottom of this, there's going to be quite a story to tell."

They watched him leave, and Max fought the desire to chase after him and force him to answer more questions. He was worried about Laney, who was crumpling and smoothing a napkin on the tabletop. "Do you think he's telling us the truth?"

"I don't know. I'll check out his place of business and dig up anything else I can find on him when we get back. His story could support Nolan's about the white car he found at the junkyard."

"If Ancho covered up the crime, and he thinks I can remember the accident and somehow incriminate him, why not just kill me?"

Max swallowed hard. "Peterson may have it all wrong. We're not sure he can be trusted."

Laney spoke slowly, her tone wooden. "Ancho said there were people who didn't want me to compete. People, he said." She stared at the ball of napkin in her hand. "People besides Trevor Ancho? Who?"

The sudden rush of fear in her face struck

at him. He gathered her close to his chest and pressed his mouth to her ear. "I won't let anything happen to you, Laney. I promise." Over the top of her head, he could not believe his eyes as he watched Trevor Ancho amble into the coffeehouse.

THIRTEEN

Laney felt Max's arms tighten around her. "Ancho's here," he breathed into her ear. The name started tremors rushing through her body. "Lean against me. We'll hope he doesn't notice you."

He couldn't hurt her in this very public place, yet her heart still pounded as she sneaked a peek. Ancho was dressed in jeans and a jacket, a knit cap on his head. He made genial small talk with the barista, whom he knew by name, and paid for his coffee—large, black, with room. As he stopped to pour in milk and stir the drink, he gazed around the crowded shop. Was it her imagination that his attention landed on Tanya, Beth and Jackie for a moment longer? Lingering there with something more than casual interest? Slowly, nonchalantly,

he turned toward the booth where Max and
Laney sat huddled.

Raising the coffee to his mouth, a smile
curved across his face as he looked at them.
Fear shifted abruptly to something else and
she sat up, tossed her hair away from her
eyes and looked straight back at him, as if
he was a competitor she was ready to defeat
on the ice. Mind games—she was plenty familiar with those. He beamed a genial smile
at her, making no move to either approach
or leave.

"I'm going to go talk to him," Max muttered angrily.

"No." She clamped a hand on his arm.
"He's well-known here, and we're the strangers. No one will believe he's doing anything
but enjoying a cup of coffee in his favorite
shop."

Max's nostrils flared, his jaw tight. "He's
taunting you."

"Let him bring his A game, then," she said,
not releasing him. "I've been baited by competitors from all over the world. He hasn't
got anything on them."

"Way to go, Birdie," he murmured, the

sheen of admiration in his glance making her warm inside. "I knew that training was worth something."

She continued to watch as a skinny man in a black apron approached to tidy up the milk station. Ancho greeted him with a slap on the back and a warm smile. They talked quietly, Ancho seeming to listen attentively as the man wiped the counter and left.

Ancho once again turned his attention to Laney. One more sip, another enigmatic smile over the rim of his mug. He winked at her.

I'm watching you.

So watch. Watch me beat you at your own game.

Ancho greeted a few more of the seated customers as he headed back to the door. Pausing on the threshold, he took a last lazy sip and left. She heaved a sigh of relief, and Max's rigid posture relaxed.

"Sizing us up?" Max suggested.

"Not sure." She stretched as she stood, muscles complaining from her earlier training. "I'm going to visit the little skater's room and then we'd better go."

"All right. I'll check outside and see if Ancho has really left." He got up, lips still pursed in that way that meant he was turning over the interview with Peterson in his mind. On impulse she got on tiptoe and kissed the frown line on his forehead, not caring if Beth or the others saw her do it. "You're the only person I'd want next to me through this, Max."

His mouth twitched. "We'll do more than get through it, we'll ride it all the way to the finish line. Together." The last word was light and delicate like a snowflake falling from his lips, or a paper bird floating on a cool winter breeze.

She wanted to tell him that he meant so much more to her than a trainer, that he stirred emotion deep in her soul that felt, sometimes, an awful lot like love. Instead, she flashed him a smile and turned to hide the flood of tenderness that washed through her.

"See you in a minute," Max said.

She watched him push through the front door before she headed down the narrow corridor to the ladies' room.

The hazy mirror in the bathroom reflected her image back in unflattering detail. Her hair was mussed, spots of anger showed on her cheeks and there was not so much as a dot of gloss on her lips.

She dashed some water on her face and used wet fingers to plaster her hair back into some semblance of order. She was reaching for a paper towel when the lights went out, plunging the room into darkness.

The one window was small and high, providing only a glimmer of light. From outside there was a clamor of voices, people moving cautiously, occasional shouts. General noises of confusion. The whole shop must be blacked out. Someone ran into a power pole? Plausible explanation, but it did not seem to calm her racing pulse.

All right. Forget drying hands. She reached for the door and pushed.

It was wedged tight. She banged on it with a flat palm. "Hey, somebody let me out."

She doubted if she could be heard by the milling patrons in the other room, but surely one of the workers would take notice. As the seconds ticked by with no response, she fumbled for her phone to call Max, nearly crying out in frustration when she realized she'd left it in Max's truck.

Great time to forget your cell phone, Laney. Dumb, dumb, dumb.

"Help," she shouted again, rattling the handle, which turned easily, but did not release the door. Dropping to her knees, she could not see anything impeding it, until she realized it was wedged from the other side.

Someone had locked her in.

Not someone. Ancho.

Nerves sparking, she kicked at the door hard enough to make the wood shudder, yelling until she ran out of air. When she stopped for breath she heard movement on the other side. "Is anyone out there?"

"Oh, yes," came a man's voice. "But don't you worry, I'm coming in."

Her body iced in fear. "Ancho?" she whispered.

There was no answer, only a hiss of soft laughter.

"I'm going to scream," she forced out. "Loud."

After a long pause he answered in a half

whisper with his mouth pressed to the crack in the door. "I hope so."

The fear bubbled thick inside her, over-whelming her confidence and tensing her muscles for flight. Over the hubbub outside, her screams might not make much differ-ence. Max would realize soon that she hadn't come out, but getting through the crowd would take time, and now the handle of the door was rattling.

"Ready or not," he said.

She backed up until the porcelain of the sink pressed hard against her back. She'd fight him to the last ounce of her strength, she'd fight with every fiber and sinew, but he was strong and crazy.

Think, Laney. God gave you a mind, so use it.

Only two exits, the door and the window. The door was out of the question.

In a moment she'd climbed up on the sink and unlocked the window, sliding the heavily mildewed glass aside. It left only about a ten-inch-square opening and she was not sure her muscled thighs would fit through. *If they don't, he'll be left to deal with my feet,* she thought, wishing she had those razor-sharp blades strapped to her soles at that moment. She grabbed the sill and shoved her head through. The night air stung her face and she realized the window opened up onto the back of the shop, a wood-fenced area housing a Dumpster and empty pallets. The place stank of garbage but there was no room for squeamishness. She shoved and wriggled her way until her torso cleared the window.

Almost through.

From there she began to shove and twist her way past the frame. Over her panting and the creak of the protesting sill, she heard the sound of the bathroom door opening behind her.

Max did not see Ancho's truck on the street or the side streets, neither was there any sign of a fancy sports car, though he did not think Ancho would be stupid enough to drive it. He had the Aston Martin tucked away somewhere in one of his warehouses, probably. As Max returned to the shop he saw that the interior was black except for a half-dozen cell phones turning into makeshift flashlights by the patrons. Power outage? Now? He dialed Laney's number. No answer. Pulse pounding, he jogged back to the store, navigating through a wave of people exiting the shop in stumbling fashion as if they were sleepwalking. Inside, at the end of a hallway, he saw two employees struggling with a panel, one holding a flashlight for the other.

"What's wrong?"

A young man, no more than twenty with hair pulled into a ponytail, yanked at a metal panel with a pry bar. "Some joker turned off the breakers and jammed the door to the electrical panel shut."

Some joker? He had a feeling he knew exactly who had done it by circling around the back entrance after he'd pretended to leave. Max left them to their efforts and moved as quickly as he could toward the back where Laney had gone to use the restroom. All the while his heart hammered hard against his ribs and he did not allow himself to think about the details.

Just find her.

Someone bumped into him. Tanya's face shone oddly by her cell-phone light. "Max?"

"Yeah. Where's Laney?"

"Jackie went to find her."

"Beth?"

Tanya shrugged. "Dunno. Lost track of her when she excused herself to feed the parking meter. This is weird, huh?"

She didn't know how weird. He steered her toward the exit. "Wait outside. I'll find Jackie and Beth."

Tanya held her phone in one hand and used the other to feel her way along. Max took out his phone and activated the flashlight app. There were only about a dozen people left in the shop; some sat as though a loss of power was commonplace, waiting until the lights were restored.

This blackout was anything but commonplace. He shoved chairs out of his way and moved faster.

"We're asking everyone to please leave, sir," said the skinny guy who had been cleaning up the milk station. "Just until we get the power back up."

"My friend is in the bathroom. I need to be sure she's okay."

The kid put a hand up. "She's probably outside safe and sound. I need you to go back out the front door now."

Was the guy in on it? Max straightened to full height. "I'm going to check on her, unless you think you're going to stop me."

He'd kept his tone level, his distance appropriate, but the guy got the message anyway. Shrugging, he stepped back out of the way. Max shuffled as quickly as he could to the back hallway.

He found Jackie stepping out of the bathroom, a frown on her face.

"Is Laney in there?"

"No."

His hands balled into fists. "Well, where is she?"

"It's ridiculous, but the window is open. I think it opens to the back parking lot."

Max made it to the rear exit when the lights flicked on. He shoved through the door into the back lot, relief flooding through him when he found Laney, breathing hard, smudges of dirt on her face. He ran to her.

"What happened?"

"Ancho locked me in the bathroom," she panted. "He was after me, but I climbed out the window. I think he heard people coming and gave up."

Anger and relief chased each other through his heart. "Are you hurt at all?"

"No," she said, face suddenly breaking into a glorious grin. "But he's got my footprint on his face."

He pulled her to him in a bear hug that turned into something else when he felt the shudder of her breath on his cheek. The need to protect her seemed ridiculous when she'd just outsmarted Trevor Ancho without any help from him, yet the thought that someone might harm her made him red-hot crazy. He crushed her to his chest and rubbed his face against her hair, his lips finding their way to hers and pressing a kiss there. *No one can take you away from me.* The thought seemed to come from a place inside that had nothing to do with racing or training, a feeling born somewhere far away from ice rinks and competitions.

But he knew it was not true. She could be taken away in a heartbeat or at the end of a prolonged agony that stripped her of dignity, like Robby. Their time together could come to a halt just as quickly as it had the moment the car plowed into them on that snow-shrouded road. He would not be able to do the smallest of things to change that. The dark despair that lived inside rose up to swallow the light in his soul, and he forced himself to let go of her, lips still throbbing from the kiss.

"We've got to go to the police," he said gravely.

"No. I'm not hurt, and I don't want to risk any more bad publicity that could affect my spot on the team. Besides, I'm sure no one will believe he locked me in the bathroom."

"Who locked you in the bathroom?" Jackie said as she joined them.

Beth and Tanya approached from the street in time to hear Jackie's question.

Beth laughed. "Did you forget how to unlock the door?"

Laney looked at Max, and he knew she was weighing her words carefully.

"I think someone locked me in," Laney said.

Tanya's mouth fell open. "Why would they do that?"

"I don't know. But I crawled out the window."

Jackie was looking at her strangely. "The door opened when I came to find you."

"I think the guy that did it unlocked it and came in."

Jackie's eyebrows raised nearly to her hairline. "You girls wait for me in the car," she commanded. "I'll be right there."

Tanya and Beth exchanged a look but did as they were instructed. Jackie waited until they left. She turned serious eyes on Laney. "I'm worried about you, as a coach and a friend. I've known you for a long time, and I was pleased when you made it back from your accident to compete again."

"But…?" Laney prompted.

"But I'm worried that the stress is getting to you."

"Because you think I'm making up stories, imagining things."

Jackie took a breath. "Well, if you were me, wouldn't you think the same thing? You've had nightmares since we started the season six months ago, lost track of things, accused someone of abducting you and now this." She waved a hand toward the bathroom.

"She's telling the truth," Max said.

"I want to believe that, Max, and I know you do, also. What proof do you have that we can use to show to the police?"

Laney bit her lip. "I don't want to involve them."

She nodded. "I understand that. I'd probably advise Beth to do the same, but I think normal people who weren't competing for an Olympic shot would advise you to do exactly that." She gave Max a pointed glance. "I think those normal people would say your mental health and physical safety are worth more than a potential gold medal."

He knew she was right. Laney should go to the police, even if it meant quitting racing, but he would not force her to do so. Was it fear that she'd end her racing career? Or worry that racing was the only thing that tied them together? Was he being respectful of her feelings or selfish because of his own?

Laney gave Jackie a hug, which the woman returned somewhat stiffly. "Thank you,

Jackie. I know you want the best for me. I'll think about what you said, but in the meantime, I'm not going to involve the police."

Jackie gave her an awkward pat. "I understand, and I won't volunteer any information, but if Coach Stan asks me directly about tonight I'm going to have to tell him, even if it makes you look bad."

"I do understand, and I don't want you to do anything that puts your job in jeopardy."

Jackie blinked and flashed a tight smile. "Thank you. If I couldn't coach, that would be bad for everyone."

They headed for the street, where Beth and Tanya stood leaning against the bumper of Jackie's Volkswagen.

Max frowned. "No parking meter?"

"What?" Jackie said.

"I thought Tanya told me Beth went to feed the parking meter before the lights went out, but you're not parked in a metered space."

Jackie's mouth twitched and she jangled the keys impatiently. "Tanya must have been mistaken."

"So she wasn't with you, then," he said lightly, "when the power went out."

"No," Jackie said. "Is there something significant in that?"

They locked eyes for a moment. He knew she would do anything for Beth just as he would do the same for Laney. At some level, this tough, competitive woman probably loved her student.

Like he loved Laney?

Thin ice, Max.

"No, nothing significant," he said. Heading for more solid ground, he ushered Laney back to his truck.

FOURTEEN

Before dawn, Laney had another nightmare that jolted her awake, sweating and shivering. The car hurtled toward them as she clutched Max's hand. In the dream she wanted to scream, to shriek out a warning so the car would stop, but she could not move, riveted to the spot and mute with terror. For that, she was grateful. At least she hadn't awakened anyone with her screams this time.

Clutching the sheets around her, she let the feelings wash over her instead of wishing them away. White car, flying snow, the driver's face. A man? A woman? Try as she would to hold on to the fleeting memories, they sifted out of her consciousness like sand through a sieve. Instinct told her the memory was the key to understanding why Trevor Ancho was stalking her and why someone had sabotaged her skate. For once she wanted to remember, and now she found she couldn't.

She threw the pillow in frustration, startling Cubby from his sleep.

"Sorry, baby," she murmured, gathering him up for a cuddle. Her mind floated back to the kiss, Max's lips against hers, the emotional connection that even now made her shiver. He was just relieved. That was all it had been. So why did every nerve in her body seem to recall the kiss in finely etched detail? Breathing deep, she blew the thoughts away. Checking the wall calendar, she confirmed that it was indeed Saturday, the day they were on their own for conditioning and workouts. Max had arranged some ice time, which would end with a practice sprint between herself and Beth.

Laney's thoughts returned to Beth as she fed Cubby. Max's question about Beth's whereabouts during the blackout at the coffee shop piqued her interest. At first it had worried her that he was paying particular notice to the girl, since Beth had taken every available opportunity to flirt with him. And why should it bother her? For one thing, she was way too young for him, on the cusp of twenty. And why would he be attracted to her? Sure she was pretty, vivacious, from a wealthy family. The list grew in Laney's mind along with an uncomfortable flutter in her stomach.

Beth was all the things Laney was not. Hip and edgy, a talented skater who could conceivably have two more chances at gold medals in her future, a girl who thrived on excitement and commanded attention from everyone she encountered. If that was what Max wanted, he was free to go after it, wasn't he?

She sat down on the edge of the bed and prayed, feeling the calm that always followed.

With a restored sense of ease, she checked her messages. One was from her father, who said he would be there for lunch with good news. She breathed a sigh of relief. Good news was something she could use, and the best news of all would be that her father was not going to do anything foolish where Ancho was concerned. She resolved to talk to him at lunch regarding the rumor that her sister mentioned about the cabin and the strange hints Peterson had dropped. It was time for full disclosure.

The second text was from Max. Meet me at ten for training at running track. M.

Ten? The text had been sent thirty minutes before, at just barely 6:00 a.m. In all their days together, Max, who rose before the sun just like she did, had never embarked on a training session any later than 7:00 a.m. Starting at the luxurious hour of ten o'clock was inconceivable.

She knew. He was going to the junkyard, and he was determined not to involve her.

"Well, I'm involved, Max," she said out loud. "So you might as well get used to it."

I'm coming with you, she messaged, even if I have to hotwire a car.

She dressed quickly and stowed a couple of snacks in her jacket pockets. Max was in the parking lot, arms folded, long frame draped against the door of his truck.

"You have no idea how to hotwire a car," he said.

"It's amazing what you can learn on You-Tube."

"Uh-huh." He sighed and opened the door for her. "Get in, if you must."

"Oh, I must," she said. "Where's Nolan?"

"We're picking him up."

They met the boy at a gas station in town. He greeted Laney enthusiastically as he hopped in. "Saw you crash. It was epic."

She laughed. "Glad I was entertaining. Lots more exciting than making it to the finish line, I suppose."

"Just like race-car driving," Nolan enthused. "Crashes are what make it interesting."

Nolan guided them to a main road that split off in different directions. Max headed south, which led them away from town, past small houses and an occasional vehicle. It promised to be a clear day, no snow in the forecast, and at the early morning hour the mountains were silhouetted in breathtaking detail as the sky turned from black to pewter. Nolan peppered them with questions about skating and competitions.

"Sounds like you've got the skating bug. Why don't you give it a shot?" Laney said. "Take some classes and try out for the junior team."

Nolan's face shuttered, fingers picking at a hole in the knee of his jeans. "Too much work."

"You don't look like someone who's afraid of work to me," she said gently. "Is it too much money?"

Max shot her a look that said he found her question too nosy.

Nolan shrugged, looking out the window.

"I know how you can make it work," she said quietly. The boy might have been herself at age fifteen, looking at the world from the outside in. If it wasn't for her father, she wouldn't have had the nerve, the means or the support to try skating. She could not help Nolan with the nerve, but she knew about a program that would help him get started, a program she and her sister had raised money to fund.

"I don't need any help," he snapped.

"Okay. If you change your mind, let me know." She scribbled her cell number on a piece of paper, and he took it grudgingly and jammed it into his pocket. Laney intended to do everything in her power to help change his mind.

The road climbed upward, and they passed pockets of blue spruce, green branches crowned with light patches of snow sparkling in the golden sunrise.

"Turn there," Nolan said, pointing to a narrow road.

Laney clutched the door frame as they bumped along the uneven surface. "How did you ever find this place?"

"I like to explore," he said. "Had a cool motorbike for a while until it busted."

"Did you come here alone? All this way by yourself?" she said.

"I'm not a child," Nolan informed her. "Been coming here since I was in grade school. School is boring, so sometimes I skip if I can get away with it."

Max drove onto an area of more level ground and navigated a series of tight turns that brought them to the perimeter of a chain link fence. They piled out. Untidy heaps of motors and rusted scrap metal poked through the snow.

"There's a gate around the side," Nolan said. "It's never locked 'cause the padlock's busted and they don't replace it." He trotted along the perimeter of the fence and gestured for them to follow. "Come on."

"I'm pretty sure this is a bad idea," Max said, trying to stop Laney from following. "Let me…"

"Too late for a thinking it out, and besides, I don't see a No Trespassing sign," she said as she followed Nolan.

"That's because most people know better," he muttered, falling in behind her.

He was right, no doubt, but the sobering thought was not enough to slow her in the slightest.

Max caught up with them at the gate. Nolan was right, it was closed, but not secured due to the rusty padlock, which had been broken off. There was no sign indicating hours of operation or even declaring the owner of the property. Shutting off the cascade of warning advice from the place inside him where common sense resided, he opened the gate and stepped through behind Nolan and Laney.

"Who runs this junkyard?" Max whispered.

Nolan shrugged. "Mostly nobody. Never seen anyone here in all the times I visited. Every once in a while there's some new stuff, but mostly nothing ever changes here."

It was some comfort to think it was an abandoned property since they were moving steadily toward trespassing. If they found anything they could get Officer Chen to come investigate properly. *A quick in and out, Max. That's all.*

There was probably nothing but worthless metal inside, but could he really turn away when there was the possibility of uncovering the truth? A flicker of pain rippled up his leg. If someone had helped the hit-and-run driver cover up the crime, as Hugh Peterson suggested, then he had to do everything in his power to find out the identity of that person. If it turned out to be Ancho, so much the better. A thin layer of dirty snow crunched under his feet as he pushed farther in.

The evidence seemed to support Nolan's

conclusion that the place was abandoned. It was more of a disordered labyrinth of junk than a well-run business, as far as he could see. He skirted a pile of hubcaps, rusted and ruined no doubt by the light coating of snow. Trailing in and out of the mess, he wondered again what exactly he hoped to find here. The white car that might have run them down? What were the chances of that exactly? A million to one.

"Watch your step, Laney," he said, pointing to a bundle of metal rods that cut across their path. On either side rose piles of stacked cars, mashed into compact bundles, most of them so old the paint color was no longer discernible. An aroma of gasoline and mildew permeated the air.

He called to the boy, who had gone ahead. "Nolan, where did you see the car? The one that had the sharpening kit inside?"

"In the shed," Nolan said, thrusting a finger. "There."

Farther back was a wooden structure, enclosed on three sides and with a sheet-metal roof. A large sliding door was open, revealing an interior full of materials they would need to be closer to identify.

Laney was already making her way toward the shed.

It wouldn't do any good to tell her to slow down. He found, in spite of the unpleasant ticking of his nerves, that he was smiling. Telling Laney to slow down was like ordering the snow to return to the clouds. Not happening, and he found something inside him warmed at the thought. Her hair was gilded by the morning sun, sparkling almost as brightly as the ice crystals, delicate fingers splayed while she worked at keeping her balance and avoiding buried obstacles.

Perfect. He did not know where the word had come from but it was true: this impulsive, forgetful, tender-hearted woman. Laney Thompson was divinely perfect in her imperfection. Divinely? As in made that way by God? He found it rang true in his soul, and with it came a wave of terror.

What God made breathtakingly perfect, He also took away.

Pain struck at him hard and brutal. The

only way to dull that vicious agony was to keep her safe…and away from his heart.

Max quickened his pace, listening as he did so for any sound of someone else in the junkyard. He thought he caught a noise, the clink of metal, and he froze, ears straining for an endless minute, but nothing materialized. In spite of the hairs that prickled on the back of his neck, he forced himself to move carefully into the shed, stopping one more time before he entered to listen again.

Still nothing.

The old steel door had rusted into the open position a long time ago by the looks of it, allowing a small amount of snow to collect in the threshold.

Towering piles of junk rose nearly to the ceiling of the space, interlocking rods of rusted metal, broken car doors, engine parts and grilles of every description. Screws and bolts littered the floor.

"It's been a while since I been here." Nolan pulled at a bent antenna, causing a miniavalanche of corroded bits to slide down.

"Don't do that," Max cautioned, surveying the massive piles above them. "This stuff weighs several tons. One wrong shift and we're going to be buried alive."

Nolan withdrew his hand, looking up at the hulking mass above them.

"So you never saw anyone here?" Max asked. "No employees or maybe somebody you've seen in town before?"

"Nope," Nolan said. "One time there were some kids messing around, but no adults. That's why I like it here. It's like my own private hideaway." He rubbed his chin. "Sorry, but I don't see that white car around anywhere. Guess somebody sold it for scrap or something."

Laney peered closely at the stacks of cars. "Maybe it's farther back," she said, squeezing between two pillars of wrecked autos.

"Don't, Laney," he said. "You're going to destabilize it."

"I'm being careful," she said, moving farther in.

The sight of her tiny form dwarfed by the massive unsteady wall was too much. This had to end before Laney or Nolan got hurt. Time to be the voice of reason, or at least try, anyway. He went to take her arm and force her out of harm's way.

"Hey," Nolan yelled. "I think I hear..."

Max reached for Laney just as a tumble of gears fell off a nearby stack. He held up an arm to shield them both as the rusted parts rained down, pinging into the smashed metal and cascading to the floor.

"I didn't make that happen," Laney said, eyes wide.

In a moment, they heard the growl as a muscular black dog appeared over the top of a low pile, teeth bared, ears flat against its head.

Max froze, clutching Laney's hand, her fingers rigid in his palm.

The dog picked its way down from the top of the pile, nose twitching. Max watched in horror as the hair on the scruff of the dog's neck raised along with the volume of his growl.

"Stay behind me," Max said to Laney, easing himself to shield her. "Nolan, walk slowly backward toward me, okay?"

Suddenly, the growls escalated into full-blown barks and the dog launched itself in their direction.

FIFTEEN

Laney screamed over Max's shoulder. "Nolan!"

The boy held out both hands. She thought he was frozen in shock until he dropped to one knee in front of the dog.

Max bolted forward.

"It's okay," Nolan said, stopping him.

"Nolan, no...." Laney's mouth fell open as the menacing dog flopped over on its back and allowed the boy to scratch his belly.

"This is Chester. He's a good dog."

Heart pounding, Laney tried to find words. "I thought...I thought he was going to eat you."

Nolan laughed. "He lives up the mountain with this old retired guy and his wife, but he likes to come down here and pretend he's a guard dog. We used to play together a lot." He fished a plastic-wrapped sandwich from his pocket. "Just peanut butter, Chester. Sorry it's not salami and cheese, but I didn't know you'd be here today." He rewrapped half of the sandwich and gave the other half to the dog, who set to work on it, tail wagging.

Max heaved out a relieved sigh. "I'm glad you bonded with him."

"You were scared, weren't you?" Nolan said, smiling mischievously.

"Yes," Laney and Max said simultaneously, which set them all to laughing.

Chester finished his snack and gave Laney and Max a thorough sniffing. He regarded Laney with a touch of condescension. "I think he knows I'm a cat person. Sorry, Chester, but Cubby would not approve of you, either."

"I'd take a dog that smells like peanut butter over a cat with tuna breath any day," Max stage whispered to the animal, who rewarded him with a wet nose to the shin.

While Nolan hunkered down next to Chester and administered a thorough scratching to the adoring critter, Laney continued her search of the shed, Max accompanying her. They stayed clear of the tottering piles as best they could. Some of the vehicles had been so completely crushed it was impossible to tell what make and model they had been before they arrived at the junkyard. After twenty minutes Laney was beginning to doubt they would discover anything but a case of tetanus lurking in those twisted metal sculptures. Her feet were numb from the cold and Max's cheeks were pink along with the tip of his nose.

"I guess it was a long shot." She kicked at an eye bolt that skittered across the ground, ricocheting against the wall with an odd hollow thud. Exchanging a look with Max, she set to work pushing debris aside with her hand, uncovering the outline of a rectangular panel set into the wall.

"A door? Yes, there must be some sort of back room we didn't see at first," she breathed.

Max found a latch and yanked. There was no movement at all. "Locked?"

"Frozen shut, I think." Laney looked around for a piece of metal suitable to pry at the edges, coming up with a broken piece of pipe that suited. Both of them tugged until they felt the panel give slightly. When Max jerked at the door again, it opened with a loud squeal. He shone a small penlight into the opening. She crowded near him to see, pressing her chin into his shoulder. She'd forgotten how strong his back was, how unyielding the shoulder muscles due to his incessant workouts. Clearing her throat, she eased back a few inches. "What's in there?"

The space was a later addition to the ramshackle shed, made of newer material and sheet-rocked walls. It had to be no more than twelve feet by twelve feet with another roll-up door at the back. The cement floor was clean and the ceiling reinforced so no snow had made it in. There was nothing inside except a large object covered neatly with a tarp. It was impossible to tell in the gloom what kind of vehicle lay underneath the plastic.

Max's eyes glittered with excitement that no doubt matched her own. Finally, they'd found one piece of evidence.

He crept into the space and she followed. Laney could hardly contain her excitement.

Nolan came over to stick his head through the door, Chester trotting along at his heels. "I never saw this place before. It's like a hidden room or something. Cool."

Max fumbled in the darkness for the edge of the tarp. Laney realized she was holding her breath.

"Did you find what you were looking for?" Nolan said.

"If it's a banged-up white car, we sure did," Laney whispered.

Finally Max seized the edge of the tarp and pulled it aside.

"What?" Laney craned forward to see. "Is it the car?"

Max's eyes were wide and there was an odd expression on his face. Was it relief? Satisfaction? She could not tell.

"Take a look, Laney," he said, pulling back the tarp and exposing what lay underneath.

Max watched her quick intake of breath, the flicker of her eyes from him to the tarp and back again.

"Hey," Nolan said, squeezing into the space. "That's not a white car. What kind is that?"

Max lowered the tarp. "It's an Aston Martin, a very expensive sports car."

"Nice," Nolan said. "But who would put a car like that in here?"

"I know who," Laney murmured.

Max took a photo with his cell phone, frustrated that he could not see the rear license plate. Then he covered the car, and they exited, breath puffing in the cold air as they emerged in the shed. He wanted to sit down and think, but a sense of urgency fueled him as he herded Laney, Nolan and the dog toward the gate.

Laney insisted that they drive Chester back to his home, and Nolan accepted thank-yous and a handful of chocolate-chip cookies from Chester's elderly owners. The husband, who introduced himself as Oscar, looked closely at Max and Laney.

"What brings you up here? Not a great time of year to go hiking."

"We were looking for something, and Nolan told us about the junkyard."

"What exactly were you looking for?"

"An old car," Max said. "Didn't find it, though." He said goodbye before the old man could ask any more questions and headed back to the truck.

Max drove a few miles, pulled over and dialed Officer Chen.

There was a long, disbelieving silence on the officer's end, and Max emailed him the photo he'd taken. Chen agreed to both investigate the shed after a scheduled meeting and uncover the identity of the property owner. Chen also commanded him in no uncertain terms to get off the property without delay.

"Yes, we're leaving right now," Max said. "I promise."

Laney was nearly bouncing on the seat in excitement. "Now there's proof."

Max didn't answer.

She touched his arm. "Isn't there? What are you worrying about?"

"We were trespassing, which Chen wasn't thrilled about, but more than that I'm just thinking that Ancho is clever. I'm wondering how he's going to try to explain his way out of it."

"I have faith in the truth," she said.

Once again, he wished he could share her

sunny outlook. Nolan returned and piled into the truck.

"Man, this was the best day ever. Got to see Chester, uncovered a sweet race car and I didn't even have to clean my room."

Laney gave him a raised eyebrow. "It's only a little after eleven. You'll be home in time to clean your room."

Max eased the truck back toward the main road. He listened to Nolan and Laney chattering away and marveled at the easy flow of conversation. So much of his life was steeped in silence, or trapped in racing and training details he'd never realized that joy might be found in mundane day-to-day life. Why should it be so, when they were engaged in a battle against Ancho and a raft of competitors vying to take away Laney's dreams of gold? He didn't know, but he allowed himself to savor the lightness of it, the sparkling moment that seemed to fill the crammed interior of his truck just then.

He pulled over in the parking lot of a fast-food joint. "Come on. I'll buy you some lunch, since you fed half of yours to Chester."

Nolan's huge grin confirmed that Max had made the right choice. Laney stared at him.

He gave her an innocent look. "What?"

"You've never set foot in a fast-food place in all the years I've known you. Not one time. Fast food means slow racing, isn't that your slogan?"

"Yeah, well, I guess there's more to life than racing, right?"

She blinked and offered him a silvery laugh that traced effervescent trails inside of him. They'd found proof that could incriminate Ancho and along the way they'd shared an adventure with a kid and a goofy dog. For some reason that he could not explain, he did not want that adventure to end.

"Who are you, and what have you done with Max Blanco?"

He wasn't sure about either question, so he got out and opened the door for her. She hopped down and took his hand. Nolan was already inside, selecting the largest meal from the menu.

He and Laney went with salads but Laney could not resist adding a small chocolate milkshake and two straws. "I'll only be half as slow if you share it with me," she said.

They sat down to eat. The restaurant was still relatively uncrowded, only a few patrons enjoying their early lunches. A man in working clothes shuffled in and ordered. Max was listening to Nolan tell a joke. The man helped himself to a soda and stood sipping it, waiting for his order.

There was nothing unusual about him; he was middle-aged, his face tanned and lined. Paint splatters on his pant legs showed him to be in the trades. His gaze wandered to the windows, across the tables and landed, just for a moment, on Max, Laney and Nolan. He gathered up his to-go order and shuffled out.

Max watched him traverse the parking lot and climb into a pickup. He sat for a moment, making a call before he drove away.

Laney was deep in the throes of carbohydrate ecstasy. She sighed. "I know milkshakes are bad, but why do they taste so good?"

He couldn't help but laugh as he declined the final sip. "You go ahead, but you have to know that will get you an extra mile on the treadmill tonight." His gaze wandered to the window again.

"Totally worth it," she said. "What are you looking at?"

He shook his head. "Nothing. Enjoy your milkshake, Laney. We've got a race to win."

Laney suited up at the arena for her race with Beth. A warm-up, followed by a five-hundred-meter sprint to practice their cornering—at least that was how they were all talking about it. She saw Coach Stan and his assistant talking quietly on the far end of the ice. They all wanted to see if she could do it. In light of all the recent events, she could understand their doubt about her level of commitment and drive. Deep down she felt a surge of optimism that Ancho was soon to be sidelined.

She was sitting on a bench at the edge of the ice to unpack her skates when her father joined her.

She kissed him, noting the dark circles under his eyes.

"You said you had good news, Dad. Let's hear it."

He sighed. "I might have been premature in that."

Max stood a few feet away, scribbling on a clipboard. Dan gestured him over. "You should probably hear this, too. I know it hasn't been fair to ask you to keep training when I haven't paid you in three months."

Max avoided Laney's eyes. "You didn't ask. I volunteered."

Laney felt her stomach sink.

"Mr. Thompson," Max said after a hesitation. "I know this is important, but can we delay this conversation just until Laney's raced? I need her head to be in the game, and I think you want that, as well."

"Of course. I should have realized that. I'll wait here and we can talk after."

Laney gritted her teeth. "No. You are more important to me than my racing. Tell me now."

Her father patted her hand. "Max's right. I'll wait."

"No, Max is not right." She fired a look at him. "He's a brilliant trainer, but he is not going to make me put skating first right now. You are my priority. I love you and I'm not setting one blade on the ice until you tell me what's going on."

He laughed, a dry, sad sound. "Now, that's a look I've seen before. All right, but I want to start by saying you are under no circumstances to stop racing, do you hear me?"

She braced herself for the blow she knew was coming. "Please, Dad."

He scrubbed a hand over his unshaven chin. "After your accident, after we lost our sponsor, things were tight. When you recovered enough to start training again, there wasn't enough money to go around, even though you worked to help out with the costs."

"I knew the financial picture wasn't great, but, Dad…"

"Listen, Laney, before I lose the nerve to tell you."

She clamped her lips closed.

"At the World Championships three months ago, I was approached by a man who offered to loan me money. He was a local businessman, a racing fan who was moved by your situation, or so I thought. I…" He sighed and chewed his lip. "I borrowed a sum with the agreement that I'd pay it back by the first of this month, only I couldn't." He looked at his hands. "The cab shop was slower than I thought."

"Oh, Dad."

He held up a finger. "Don't interrupt. I couldn't pay it back, and the man became angry and threatening."

"The police..." Max started.

"Don't you see? I couldn't tell them I'd borrowed from a loan shark," he said. "Laney's reputation would be ruined. She'd be shamed off the training team and her skating career would be over."

"It was Ancho, wasn't it?" Laney forced herself to say.

He nodded, and her mind spun in helpless circles. "Oh, Daddy."

"I've got until the end of the week or he'll let it slip to the officials." He coughed. "Ancho tried to rough me up, but that didn't work. Then..." Her father's voice broke. "Then when I heard what he'd done to you, I went to him with everything I had and told him to stay away from you or I'd go to the police no matter what. He just laughed and told me to go ahead, that no one would believe me just like they didn't believe you."

She squeezed his hand. "You made a mistake. We've got to tell the police."

"Is that why you didn't want us talking to Hugh Peterson?" Max said. "Did he know about your loan?"

"Yes. I don't know how, but he knew. He came and asked me about it. I didn't want him to tell you so I tried to keep him away."

"It's after two o'clock," Jackie said, skating up to them. "Are we racing or not?"

Laney was still too tongue-tied to talk, but Max spoke up. "Sure, couple more minutes."

She nodded and skated to the far end where Beth was practicing.

Max looked out over the ice. "Do you think Ancho had something to do with messing up Laney's skates?"

"I don't know. I wouldn't put it past him. Anything to scare me into getting his money back."

"That's why you arranged to sell the cabin, isn't it?" Laney said.

Her father gave a startled jerk, then nodded. "But it's not a good market right now.

It's taking longer than I thought." He sighed and her heart broke a little more. "Laney, I'm so sorry, honey. I never should have done something so stupid, but I could not stand to see your dream die. Forgive me."

She clutched him to her, grief so thick it nearly choked off her breathing. "My dream is not worth this, Daddy."

He pulled her away, tears filling his eyes. "I'll find a way to pay him by the end of the week."

"How much do you owe him?" she whispered.

"Thirty thousand dollars," he said with trembling lips.

The figure whirled in her brain. Where would they find that much money? And what would happen to her father if he didn't? But the Aston Martin, it would be enough to take Ancho down. Wouldn't it?

Max was talking quietly. "Put on your skates, Laney. You've got a drill to do."

She glared at him. "I can't race. My father is in trouble, Max."

Her father grabbed her hands and squeezed them until she gasped.

"Laney, please don't let this all be for nothing. There's a God-breathed reason you're here, why you and your sister came into our lives and why you have a passion for this sport. It's going to lead you to something in your life that you were meant to do. Maybe a medal, maybe not, but you have to do it."

"No, Dad." She shook her head and freeing her fingers, unzipped her skin suit. "I need to help you. We've found some proof that Ancho really did abduct me. I'll meet with the police and they'll arrest him."

"Laney," he whispered, catching up her hands once again. "Race for me, for your stupid old father who threw away everything to see you fly across that ice."

"Daddy..."

Coach Stan glided up to the benches and leaned his forearms on the edge. "Is there a problem? Race time was ten minutes ago."

Laney looked from Max to her father.

"Do it, Laney. Please," he whispered. His face was pale and sunken around the lips and eyes. The love there shimmered far brighter than any mistake he had ever made.

After what felt like a very long time, she

sighed. "Be there in two seconds, Coach." She zipped up her suit and laced on her skates. Both Max and her father looked supremely relieved and Coach Stan left. "I'll race, but I'm going to help you out of this mess, Dad, whether you like it or not."

Max came close to her as she stepped onto the ice. "Now's the time to see what you're made of, Laney. Mental toughness." He handed over her gloves.

"Mental toughness." She gave her father one more look and she hoped he'd see in there the love that was brimming over in her heart, along with the sorrow at what he'd done for her.

SIXTEEN

Through sheer force of will, Max kept his mind on the race, shoving thoughts of Ancho and Dan Thompson's disastrous choice to the background. He noticed Diane in the stands chatting via the Bluetooth device in her ear. It did not look like an idle conversation, but he was glad to see her click off and lean forward in anticipation of the race. Most of the athletes were also gathered in the seats, eager to see a head-to-head competition.

This would indeed be a test of Laney's mental toughness after hearing Dan's news. Could she actually leave it all on the benches and focus on the race?

Plant the point of your blade.

Laney dug the tip into the ice and crouched low, arms crooked, one in front and one behind. Classic race stance.

Explosive start.

The bell sounded and Laney took off like a rocket, charging forward with short, quick strides. But as they smoothed out into longer gliding strokes, Beth quickly assumed the first position.

Not a problem. What separated the best in the world from the merely good skaters was the turns, and Laney, when she was on, was a master. Today she did not disappoint. Her gloved hand down for support, she created as much pressure as she could with her blades against the wet ice. Three laps to go.

You've got it, Laney. Pride tingled his nerves, as much for her courageous spirit as for her perfect race form.

Laney stayed comfortably in second place, waiting, he knew, for Beth's confidence or strength to wane just the slightest bit. Laney was looking for the slot. At the beginning of the last turn, she found it. His position in the stands allowed him to see Laney turn up the speed and pass on the straightaway, but as they struggled into the corner, he saw Beth reach out and give Laney's hip a push. Patently illegal. No contact allowed on the corners.

His breath caught, but Laney adjusted quickly, not allowing the bump to throw off her technique. Digging hard, chest heaving with the effort, Laney continued her relentless pace in the last lap and skated easily to the finish in first place.

Outwardly, he kept a tranquil smile, inside he was shouting with jubilation. She'd showed the coaches and the other team members who had gathered to watch that she was indeed a world-class competitor who had just skated a flawless race and beat a girl seven years her junior. And she'd shown herself that she had the spirit to put everything behind and grind it out to the finish line.

For a moment, he felt the barest flicker of shame that he had not done the same himself. Blaze, the champion, had let his injury end his career but more significantly, he'd let it define him.

Shaking off the melancholy thoughts, he joined her as she stepped off the ice and put on her guards, giving her a hug so tight her hammering heartbeat seemed to transfer itself into his own body. "Now, that's skating, Birdie," he said, coming close, and somehow his lips touched the delicate shell of her ear.

She grinned at him. "See? I still got it."

"Yes, you do," Diane Morrison said, climbing down the stairs to the bottom level. "Doesn't look like you've lost anything since you've been away. That was poetry in motion."

Beth clomped off the ice, breath heaving. "Nice race, Laney."

"You, too," Laney gasped, giving Beth a hug.

Beth grinned. "I can't believe you actually pulled it off."

"In spite of the bump," Max could not stop himself from saying.

Beth unzipped her skin suit. "What bump?"

"The bump you gave her at the second corner," Jackie said. "You know better."

"It's short track," Beth said with a shrug. "The five hundred meters is four laps of crazy, every woman for herself. If she can't handle a little bump, then she shouldn't be racing."

Diane laughed delightedly. "She gets that attitude from me, I'm afraid."

Jackie did not smile. "She needs to win the right way or she'll always know she didn't earn it."

Diane's chuckle died away. "And isn't that your job, to make sure she earns it? I'm paying you pretty good money to make sure there's nothing between her and first place on the podium."

"I do my job. Your daughter needs to do hers."

"I expected better from her this close to the qualifiers. Maybe she needs to do it with another coach," Diane said.

Jackie's chin went up, the lights glinting on her pale hair. "Do you think that would really be a wise thing to do?"

Diane's face went hard as stone. "Rest assured that I'm not burdened by sentimentality or obligation like others are. I'm only interested in results. I'll do what's necessary."

"Mom," Beth said, her tone pleading. "I'll work harder. It's my thing, not Jackie's. I've been lazy, and I'll do better."

Diane flicked a look at her daughter and then turned on her heel and left the arena.

Beth turned to Jackie. "She's grumpy, that's all. It makes her cranky to be away from work. Let's look over the tapes, and I'll work on whatever you want me to."

Jackie allowed Beth to touch her hand. It was the first time Max had seen any kind of physical contact between them, and then Jackie pulled away.

They made their way to Dan, who clasped Laney close to his chest. "Seeing you do that, skate that well, it makes me think everything will turn out all right."

Laney did not look convinced, but she went to the changing room while Max and Dan went over the notes from the race. Dan rubbed at his temples. "I am going to pay you your back salary, Max, just as soon as I can sell the cabin. Ancho will get his money and you'll get yours."

Max didn't like being lumped into the same sentence as Ancho, but he held his tongue.

"I've been thinking about the whole situation, you borrowing from Ancho. Does it seem odd to you that Ancho would approach you about money? Doesn't it usually work the other way around with loan sharks?"

Dan grimaced. "I don't know. Never in all my wildest dreams would I have even imagined myself borrowing money from a guy like that, but he seemed so earnest—he knew all about the accident. He said he figured we had earned a break after what happened."

Max frowned. "Did he tell you anything specific about the accident? Something that he shouldn't have known about?"

"No." Dan's eyes clouded with worry. "Are you thinking he knows who hit you?"

Max considered sharing what Hugh Peterson had divulged, but he thought it might be more than the man could take to know he'd made a deal with a guy covering for the hit-and-run driver. "Just thinking out loud. I know you'll pay me when you can. I'm in this for more than the money."

Dan looked closely at him. "I know that. I've always known it. That's why I hired you to train Laney."

Max sighed. "I was afraid… Sometimes it occurred to me, that you might have chosen me because you pitied me."

A smile lit the tired corners of Dan Thompson's face. "Son, I chose you because you care about my daughter, not just because of whatever medals wind up hanging around her neck. You need someone like that to stand by you when you're on that podium and someone to hold your hand when you don't make it to the winner's circle." He closed his eyes for a moment. "I had that in Linda. And my girls have that in me. I may have messed things up for now, but that will never change." Tears glittered in his eyes. "I just wish I hadn't been so dumb. I won't ever forgive myself. God blessed me with two beautiful girls, and I let them down. I'm a terrible provider."

Max watched the tears slide down Dan's cheeks. He stood awkwardly, feeling an unsteady tide of emotion wash through him. "Seems like Laney would say God made you more than just a provider."

Dan started, then his eyes opened wide and he smiled. "I can see that I did one thing right when I hired you."

Max didn't understand the warmth he felt inside, nor the curious way Laney's comment circled in his mind, her bizarre view that racing was only a small piece of what he was meant to see, to be.

He was relieved when Laney showed up, changed into her workout gear for the rest of the day's training, cheeks still flushed petal pink from her exertions. "Ready to hit it hard?"

The smile she flashed at them both disappeared rapidly. Looking behind him, Max saw Officer Chen striding through the arena.

Chen wore street clothes, and for that, Laney was grateful. At least he didn't attract as many curious glances from the bystanders. Her father's face pinched in anxiety. She realized he did not want her to reveal his debt to Ancho, but she knew if it came down to her father's safety, she would swallow the risk and tell him everything.

"Did you find the car?" she said eagerly.

Chen held up a calming hand. "First off, the property is indeed owned and operated by Trevor Ancho. I confirmed that with him before I did my investigation. According to him, it's left unattended most of the time as he's moved on to other interests. I should add that he was cooperative and genial."

Genial. Right. "And?" She did not see in his face what she hoped for.

"And I was on my way out there an hour after I hung up with you. It's a good thing you told me about Chester. I brought a roast-beef sandwich," Chen said with the ghost of a smile.

Max stood motionless, eyes riveted on Chen. "Is it enough proof to corroborate Laney's story? Can you arrest him?"

Chen hesitated. "No."

"Why not?" Laney snapped. "What else can you possibly need?"

"The car." Chen gave her a hard look. "There was no Aston Martin or any other car in that room behind the shed. It was completely empty."

Laney heard a buzzing in her head. "How could it be empty? We saw a car, three of us, not more than a few hours ago. Max took a picture. Ancho must have moved it."

"Your picture shows the front end of a sports car, no plates showing, in a darkened area that could be anywhere. I spoke to the couple who live up the mountain, Chester's owners. They didn't notice anyone moving vehicles to and from the property."

"I can't believe this," Laney said. Her father squeezed her shoulder with a calming hand, but it did nothing to soothe her. "What can we do now? He wins at every heat."

The officer's lips thinned into a hard line. "Let me lay this out straight for you. Trevor Ancho is clean, as far as I can tell. He's got an alibi for the time you say you were abducted and he doesn't own an Aston Martin. What's more, he's an excellent citizen who has helped out with plenty of civic causes and donations. He let me onto the property when he didn't have to, and he's been nothing but cooperative. Helped build the play structure in town that my kids enjoy. In other words…"

"In other words," Max broke in. "You think we're making this all up to slander the guy. Why would we?"

Chen shifted. "Maybe because Mr. Thompson here owes him money."

Laney heard her father gasp. "How did you know that?" she managed to say.

"He told me he loaned your father a sum of money to help with your training costs, and Mr. Thompson has had difficulty paying it back. Ancho says he is perfectly willing to wait for repayment, so if these..." he gestured with his hands "...these accusations are in some way an attempt to escape the debt, you don't have to worry."

"They're not," Laney almost shouted, drawing attention from three male skaters warming up on the ice. She lowered her voice. "They're not accusations. Ancho loaned money to my father, and now he's pressuring him to pay it back. He's physically threatened both of us. Can't you see that?"

Her father's face had gone ashen, his mouth partly open as he panted for breath. "It's true, Officer. I borrowed money, and Ancho has been threatening me to repay. He's a loan shark."

"At the present time, I see no evidence of that. No car, no witnesses who say that he's threatened anyone, not one shred of evidence that he's in the business of loaning out money. You're the only one who seems to be in debt to him, as far as I can ascertain."

"He's not who he pretends to be," her father said, jaw clenched. "I should have said something earlier. It's my fault."

"No, Dad. You tried to help." She gripped his hand, which felt hot in her fingers. "So you're saying there is nothing we can do here?"

"I'm saying you need to take care of your own business and stop harassing Mr. Ancho before you wind up at the wrong end of a slander suit." Chen gave them all a final look and walked away.

"This is a nightmare," Laney whispered. They went to the benches and sat. Max unzipped his duffel and handed Laney a bottle of water.

"Drink," he commanded. "You need to hydrate."

She chugged the water until it was half gone, handing some to her father, who was sweating in spite of the cool temperature. Ancho was genial and cooperative. Laney Thompson was a crazy person trying to slander him. What was happening? Her world was spinning out of control. She didn't notice Tanya approach, skating up to the edge of the ice, ready for her own turn at a practice race.

"Hey, Laney. Good race," she said. "I…" Her words trailed off, mouth opened into an O of surprise.

"What's wrong?" Max said.

She was staring into his open duffel bag, at the sharpening kit that Nolan had found. "How did you get my sharpening kit?"

"It's yours?" Max said.

"Yeah, that's my red tag around the handle. Keeps me from picking up the wrong one. It's been missing for a while. Where did you find it?"

Max looked at Laney, who could only manage a small nod.

He cleared his throat. "A friend of ours found it in the junkyard, inside a white car, a car that might be the one that hit us."

Tanya's face went pale, then flushed an unhealthy red. For a moment, Laney thought her legs might give out underneath her and send her down hard on the ice.

She was wrong. Tanya remained standing, terror in her face.

It was Laney's father who grasped his shirtfront, gasping, and slid off the bench onto the concrete arena floor.

SEVENTEEN

Except for the colors of the hard-backed chairs and the bland watercolor prints on the wall, it could have been the same hospital where Max had spent so many months trying to stave off the inexorable march of his brother's disease. His hands went to his pockets, the craving for paper and scissors strong. He forced his palms onto his lap.

"Can I get you anything at all?" he asked.

Laney did not stop pacing long enough to answer. "No, thank you."

Her tone, void of expression, chilled him. Though he wanted to stay silent, to shroud himself in a hush that would protect against the memories that rankled inside, he could not stand to see her that way.

He got up and joined her as they walked the length of the corridor, considering what to say. He would not offer any of the mean-ingless platitudes that he'd heard so many times. *Your father is going to be okay. He's strong. We just have to keep a positive attitude.*

None of those had been true for Robby. And they might not be for Laney's father. So what could he offer? How could he comfort?

"I'll be right back," he said.

She didn't answer as he headed away, returning shortly and taking her hand to guide her to the chair next to him. "I want to show you something."

She sat, eyes dull and terrified, but watching him nonetheless.

He took out the miniscissors he'd bought at the gift shop, though he'd had to purchase an entire travel sewing kit to get one. The cashier had been nice enough to give him the paper. The pain that he did not want to feel surged again in his heart, but he forced his fingers to work anyway. Carefully he folded the paper and started the series of precise cuts, each one bringing back a flash of his brother.

"What did you make today, Max?"

"A dog."

"That's good. Make me a dinosaur next, okay?" said the little boy, struggling to move against the net of tubes and monitors that kept him prisoner on the hospital bed.

"What is it going to be?" Laney asked.

He blinked hard. "You'll see."

Robby would often ask the same.

"What's it gonna be, Max?"

"You'll see."

His fingers, it seemed, did not want to re-visit those memories with each snip, yet he forced them to do the work, the silver blades dancing in and out of the fragile white paper. He cut and notched, the grief running silent and strong inside until he'd finished and handed her the tiny square.

She opened it.

A dinosaur. Her smile unfurled slowly like a sunrise. She peeked over the top of the paper at him, reaching out a finger to trap the single tear that he had not realized was there on his cheek.

"My brother..." he croaked, and cleared his throat. "My brother liked dinosaurs." He could not speak anymore.

"Your precious brother." She clung to his

hand, eyes shimmering with emotion, and prayed for them both. He let the words trickle through his mind. Healing. Peace. Love so deep it transcended the earthly limits of life. Soothing and slowing, that tide of grief ebbed just enough to make it bearable.

He squeezed her fingers. How was it possible that here in the hospital, where he was supposed to be comforting Laney, he found himself so profoundly eased in his own spirit? It was too much.

He felt like running down the corridor and slamming out of those hospital doors. Instead, he stayed still, listening to her every word, her every breath, feeling his own heart break and mend itself together in an endless cycle carried on each syllable.

When she was done, she kissed his cheek and looked again at the dinosaur, smiling as she fingered the slender neck and pointed tail.

There was a sound of hurrying feet and he saw a stockier, darker version of Laney bearing down on them. Jen Thompson had arrived.

Shamefully, he felt relieved to pocket his

scissors and move discreetly away to allow them some private time. Jen and Laney embraced, crying, sharing bits and spurts of conversation in between the onslaught of emotion. He wished that his brother had lived, that they could have walked through life together like Laney and her sister. After Robby died, he'd decided not to walk, but to race through life alone. The choice had cost him more than he'd understood until just that moment.

After a while, Laney wiped her face and they greeted Max.

Jen gave him a hug. "Good to see you again, Max. Thanks for being here for my sister."

He realized, painful though it was, there was no place on earth he would choose to be except for right there. He offered to get them coffee or food, which they were in the process of declining when a doctor in green scrubs came out to deliver his report.

Laney clutched Jen's hand and then reached for his, her fingers rigid in his own.

"Your father has had a heart attack," the doctor said. He explained that there had been damage to the muscle, causing something called cardiogenic shock resulting in an insufficient blood flow throughout his body. "We're treating him with blood thinners now and we'll see if that stabilizes him."

"What if it doesn't?" Laney whispered. "What then?"

His tone was soothing. "We have confidence that it will. The next twenty-four hours will be a wait-and-see phase. You are welcome to stay with him for a while, but it's best that he be allowed to rest undisturbed."

The doctor excused himself. Laney and Jen were escorted to Dan's room by a nurse, Max following at a distance. He waited at the door while they went in, catching only a glimpse of Dan, pale and wearing an oxygen mask, eyes closed.

The girls settled in next to him, one on either side, crooning softly to their father. Max's own heart ached at the sight of their worried faces. Laney looked up and tiptoed over to him.

"I'm going to stay here for a while."

"I know," he said. "You have my number. Call me when you want me to pick you up or if there's anything I can do for either one of you."

She nodded, suddenly embracing him in a tight hug that sent his heart racing.

"Laney, I wish I could do something."

"You have, more than you know." She paused, heaved out a sigh and detached herself. "We can talk about training later."

He nodded, stepping away. Training. Of course. Since he'd entered the hushed confines of the hospital, he'd forgotten that he was her trainer. Whatever had happened back in the hallway, whatever feelings had taken over, were safely secured in the dark place deep inside. "Take care, Laney."

She had already turned back to her father.

Max drove slowly back to the arena, fingers drumming on the steering wheel. Without an athlete to put through the workout regimen, he was at a loss. *Find something to do, something you can fix.* The only thing that would seem to be of any help was to seek out Tanya and get to the bottom of the sharpening-kit mystery. The men's team was training hard on the ice when he returned, but there were no women to be seen.

Back at the weight room he found Jackie and Stan poring over binders full of racing information.

"How's Dan?" Stan asked, his forehead creased with concern.

"He's being treated for a heart attack. They aren't sure about the extent of the problem yet."

Jackie nodded. "So terrible that it happened now, when she was so close."

He raised an eyebrow. "Was? Laney hasn't dropped out of competition."

It was Jackie's turn to look surprised. "I assumed, with how close she is to her father, that she couldn't keep competing knowing he was in the hospital."

"Her father is the exact reason she won't quit."

Stan closed his binder. "Did she say that, Max? Or are you making an assumption?"

"I'm not the one assuming, you are." Max felt a kindling of anger. "She won't quit, so don't ace her out of a spot just yet."

He strode out, trying to decipher his own feelings. Was he offended that they didn't think she had the commitment to keep going? Or worried that deep down they were right? And at the bottom, the very core of his emotion, was the numbing fear that if she was done with racing, she was done with him, too. Tension bridling inside made him change into workout clothes for a run on the track. It would be good to clear his mind, and he'd have to pass right by the weight room, where he figured the women must be training.

Tanya was riding on the stationary bike when he spotted her, thin freckled face frowning in concentration.

Immediately she ducked her head and pretended not to see him.

That's not going to work, Tanya. I need some answers.

For an hour, Jen and Laney watched their father sleep, wiping his brow with a damp cloth and quietly asking each other unanswerable questions before they got down to the particulars.

"Did you finish your finals?" Laney said, keeping her voice low.

"Yes." Jen broke into a smile. "Aced them."

Laney gave her a soft high five. "When do you need to be back?"

"Not for a week. Dad timed his heart attack just right," Jen said, mouth twisting in grief. She cleared her throat. "I'm going to stay here until you qualify for the team. Then we'll play it by ear."

Laney sighed. "Jen, I'm not sure that's going to happen. There are some things I need to tell you." She launched into the whole story, interrupted twice by nurses coming to check vital signs on their father. When she was done, Jen's eyes were wide.

"I had no idea Dad was in such trouble. And you, too. What are we going to do?"

Laney got up and prowled the room. "I think I should quit." The words seemed to tear at her mouth as they left her lips. "Then the pressure is off. Dad can pay back the money when he can. Trevor's got nothing to hold over him—there's no risk of the committee booting me off because I'll take myself out of it."

Her sister's brown eyes glimmered and the room fell into silence broken only by the beep of monitors and the squeak of rubber-soled shoes on the corridor outside. "Laney, if you quit, Dad will never forgive himself."

"What choice is there?"

"Only one," she said, quietly, sitting stiff backed in the chair. "You're going to race. Dad sacrificed everything to give us a chance at a normal life. He could be retired and spending his free time fishing at the cabin, but he kept up the business and borrowed that money so we could chase our dreams. If you quit, then he's failed."

"I'm not sure."

"Yes, you are. Deep down, you don't want to quit, do you?"

She toyed with the window blinds.

"Do you?" her sister said again.

"No," Laney admitted. "I don't. I can win. I want to win."

"Of course. We had a terrible childhood, but living like that taught us not to quit. Dad always said it made us brighter, like fire does to gold and hardships do for our faith. Are you going to prove him right or wrong?"

"It's not just about me," Laney groaned. "You are affected by my decision, too."

Jen got up and took Laney by the shoulders. "You're right, so make sure that you don't let us down by quitting."

The phone buzzed in Laney's pocket and she excused herself to answer it in the corridor.

"It's Hugh Peterson. I need to talk to you, right away."

"I can't," Laney said, explaining about her father.

Hugh blew out a breath. "I'm sorry about your dad, but I've got some information that will explain why Ancho's been hounding you. We can nail him and get him off your father's back for good. That should be the best medicine of all, shouldn't it?"

Laney's heart ticked up a notch. "Tell me over the phone."

"Can't right now. In an hour. My condo." He rattled off an address.

"Hugh, what is this about? I'm not going…" She realized she was talking to dead air.

She looked up to find Jen standing in the doorway. "Is that about the situation with Dad?"

"It could be. I think I'd better go find out."

"With Max, right?"

Laney frowned. "I shouldn't involve him any more than he already is." She shot a look at her father. "And I don't want to leave Dad."

"I will stay with him every minute, and you will take Max because it would be dumb to do otherwise."

"And they say I'm the outspoken one," Laney said.

Jen shrugged. "Dad didn't raise any shrinking violets."

"No he didn't," she said, hugging her sister and giving her father a gentle kiss.

She called Max and waited, stalking in impatient stretches across the admissions lobby until he arrived a half hour later. As she climbed into the truck, she was surprised to find that the sun was low in the sky. Nearly a full day had passed since they'd headed out of town to the junkyard.

Max let her do the talking, engine idling as he listened. "I'm glad you called me," he said finally.

"My sister would have had my head if I tried to go it alone."

"Your sister is pretty smart."

"Yeah." She tried to drag her mind from

the hospital room to the situation at hand. "I wish I knew what Hugh wanted to talk to me about." She worked the zipper of her jacket up and down. "Did you find out anything from Tanya?"

He grimaced. "When I got close, I was mobbed by a bunch of girls wanting to know how you were, and by the time I took care of that, Tanya was gone."

"She didn't have anything to do with the crash, Max. None of the girls did. They wouldn't cover up something like that."

He didn't answer.

She fought the urge to get out of the truck and sprint alongside it, anything to drain some of the frenetic energy from her body. "Jen says I shouldn't quit."

His head jerked a bit in her direction, but he immediately resumed focus out the front windshield.

She waited for his question but it didn't come. "I'm not sure if I should stay in or not. What do you think?" He would say, of course, that nothing should stop her from racing, not her father's heart attack, not anything.

"I think you should do what is best for your family."

She gaped. "Aren't you going to tell me not to quit?"

He sighed and suddenly he looked sad and vulnerable. "Laney, until just recently I thought racing was all that mattered. But you said it yourself, it's only a small part of who God made you to be, right?"

"Yes," she said.

"You have so many people who love you, and they're going to love you no matter if you race or not. The question is, do you feel the passion to win that gold? If the answer is yes, we train as hard as we can in the few days we have left. If not…"

"If not?"

He smiled at her. "Then, Birdie, you're free to fly somewhere else."

And so was he. She could not imagine what her life would be like without Max, but she could not skate forever, and skating was what bound them together. She thought about the single tear that had glistened on his cheek when he cut the paper dinosaur. Had he finally stopped running from the terrible sadness of his brother's death? She felt the twin pangs of happiness for him and an inkling of despair. Had she kept him prisoner, tied to her as she pursued her dreams instead of pursuing his own life outside of skating?

"I'm confused."

"Think it out and let me know."

"And if I decide not to race," she heard herself say. "What will you do?"

He turned sapphire eyes on her so brilliant that they were worlds unto themselves. "I don't know, but I think it's time for me to find out."

EIGHTEEN

The road led them into a quiet suburban neighborhood just as the sun began to sink below the hills. Trees crusted with snow lined both sides, and the streetlights flicked to life when Max turned into the long driveway of Hugh's compact, neatly tended condo. It was the farthest away from the main road, isolated from the rest by the towering pines that seemed to crowd around it. A ladder leaned against the side of the house, and paint flaked away where the owner had apparently been trying to hammer a loose shutter back into place.

Max cut the engine. Something heavy and uneasy had settled in his gut, and he wasn't sure if it was the unnatural stillness of the place or the conversation he'd just finished with Laney. As her trainer, he should have done everything in his power to convince her not to quit. He hadn't, and it bit at him that he'd let her become something other than his athlete. Dan Thompson had picked him to be more than a trainer to her, but he wondered now if his feelings had made him less.

She might quit. Walk away from the dream that sustained her.

And she might regret that loss forever, just as he did. He got out and they crunched up the path, which was obscured by a light layer of snow. Wood paneling covered the exterior of the two-story structure, an angled roof giving it a rustic appeal.

Laney knocked on the front door.

"There's a light on inside," Max said. "And one on upstairs."

"Do you hear music?"

He did. Classical piano, from the sound of it.

Laney knocked louder. "Mr. Peterson? It's Laney and Max."

They listened for the sound of footsteps but heard nothing as the dusk swallowed them in darkness.

"Maybe we're early," she said.

"Right on time. He could be in the shower or the garage and he can't hear us."

The garage was actually a three-sided carport, and Hugh's old Suburban was parked there, the hood cool to Max's touch. "Out walking?"

"He sounded urgent on the phone, desperate to meet with me. Why would he leave?"

Max's skin prickled along the nape of his neck. "Let's check the back in case he stepped outside for some air."

The porch wrapped around to the back of the house, sturdy railings enclosing a seating space that housed a rocking chair neatly covered to keep off the elements. More snow-covered trees adorned the space, along with a barbecue and bicycle tucked back against the house.

"Why would...?" She broke off as Max pointed to the sliding door, open six inches, curtains fluttering out the gap in the chill air.

"Go wait in the truck," he said. "I'm going to check things out."

"I'm going, too."

"This is not legal, Laney. We're breaking the law here and we have no idea what's waiting inside."

She nodded solemnly. "I know, but we're in this too far to leave now."

Body taut, he stepped to the opened door and listened. Still only the sound of piano music. He could see into a neat kitchen, an old tiled counter clear of clutter and a round table with a mug on it dead center. The music came from an old-type CD player sitting on a shelf just above the kitchen sink.

He stepped in. "Mr. Peterson?" he called softly.

Laney pushed through behind him. "Look," she breathed. There was a whiteboard fixed to one side of the dining room wall decorated with Hugh's scrawled print in dry-erase marker. "Beth Morrison, Diane Morrison, Trevor Ancho, Tanya Crowley, Jackie Brewster," she read, her finger resting on the last two names. "Laney Thompson, Dan Thompson."

She picked up three plastic-backed magnets from the floor. "He had things put up here."

"He's been investigating how it all fits together," Max said. "I wonder what he found out."

"And where he is now?" she asked with a shiver. She frowned. "I'm sure I didn't get the message wrong. I hope I didn't."

"You didn't," Max said, touching the Utah Jazz coffee mug. "It's still warm."

Laney's eyes widened. "So where did he go?"

"I'm going to look upstairs."

She tiptoed up the squeaky wood steps right behind him.

At the top of the stairs they found a loft with a neatly made bed. The loft opened onto a tiny bathroom, all decorated in browns, that made the place seem even gloomier.

"Mr. Peterson?" Max called again.

There was no one there.

"I'm worried, Max," Laney said.

Her face was etched with fear. "What if something bad has happened to him?"

"Let's look around a little more and then we can call the police. There could still be an innocent explanation for all this. I'm going to check his answering machine downstairs."

"Okay. I'll call my sister and check on my father." She sat on a slatted chair.

Max returned to the dining room. There was no indication that anything bad had happened to Hugh, but why would he go out and leave the door open? It did not feel right to snoop through Peterson's house, but he pressed the button on the answering machine to play back the one message.

Tanya's thin quavering voice floated through the space.

"Mr. Peterson, you contacted me before to see if I knew anything about the accident, the one that hurt Laney and Max."

Max's stomach tightened as he listened.

"I…I think I might know something. I didn't realize it before and I'm not sure it's anything so I didn't want to call the police and get anyone in trouble, but… Well, anyway, I can't talk right now but I'll call you back later, okay?" There was a click as the phone was disconnected.

His mind whirled. They weren't the only

ones looking for Hugh Peterson. Tanya had something to share with him, as well.

He felt something behind him just then, the same way he'd always been able to sense skaters stealing up on him, trying to pass. He had time enough to raise a hand to defend himself, but it did no good as the bat struck him and he crumpled to the floor, registering a fleeting glimpse of Ancho before things went black.

Jen reported to Laney that their father was resting comfortably, no change. She was not sure whether she should be pleased or dismayed. His body needed time for the medicine to work, but the waiting was agonizing.

"I called the athlete dorms, and Tanya said she'd feed Cubby for you."

Laney sighed. "Thank you. He'll get crabby without his dinner."

"You know, Laney, I'm just sitting here, staring at Dad, thinking you both have the same stubborn chin."

"Even though we're not blood related?"

She laughed, but it was a tired sound. "I've

spent the past three months studying heredity. It can influence practically everything."

Laney waited, sensing that her sister needed to say something.

"Our mom, our birth mom, I mean, was unable to handle her problems. The addiction was too strong." She paused. "Did you ever wonder, Laney, how much of her is in us?"

"She gave us our genes, but we decide what we do with them."

Jen laughed and Laney felt rewarded for easing her sister's mood for a moment. "You wouldn't pass a genetics class with that answer."

"No, but Dad would approve."

"You're right," she said quietly. "I think I'll tell him, just in case he can hear me."

Tears lashed at her eyes. "Give him a kiss for me and tell him I'll be there soon."

Jen promised she would and clicked off.

Laney got up to look out the window, surveying the bleak landscape outside. To her surprise, she found the window was not fully closed. Giving it a yank, it slid upward. Outside, a tall ladder leaned against the wood siding. Had someone entered the house that way? Or was it possible Peterson had climbed down? It would make a convenient escape, but why exit via ladder?

Only one logical reason—because someone was coming in another way, say, the back sliding door, someone who intended to do harm. She peered down into the night, trying to discern which way he might have gone, but it was too dark to make out much of anything.

Biting her lip, she started to pull herself back in through the opening when a pair of hands seized her arms from behind, trapping her in the open window.

She struggled against restraining hands. "Let go," she grunted, thrashing from side to side.

"Be careful what you wish for," Ancho said, laughing low.

Terror ricocheted through her nerve endings. "Max," she screamed.

"He won't hear you."

Her throat convulsed. "What did you do to him?"

"Let's stick to the present. I told you it would be best for you to quit racing, but here you are, not only still racing but sticking your button nose into places where it doesn't belong. Even the cops are getting tired of you."

Her torso was pinned against the window frame, arms still immobilized. Twist as she might, she could not free herself. *Max,* she screamed silently. *Max, what's happened to you?*

"If you were a good daughter, you'd be there in the hospital, at your father's bedside, not breaking and entering."

She stopped fighting for a moment to suck in a breath. "You're insane."

"Not insane," he hissed, giving her flesh a savage pinch. "Just persistent, like you."

"Help," she shouted.

"No one will hear you."

No one. "Tell me what you did to Max."

He did not seem to hear. "You're going to have a fall. It probably won't kill you, but it will break one of your legs, maybe both, possibly other bones, as well. No trials for you next week."

"Why are you doing this?" she gasped as

he levered her out the window. "I never did a thing to you."

His tone was hard as iron. "You had your shot. It's somebody else's turn."

She was frantic now. "Who are you covering for? The hit-and-run driver? You don't want me to remember, do you?"

He paused.

She knew she'd hit it. "You're scared I'll remember the accident and you want me to disappear before that happens."

"Smart lady," Ancho said.

"You did something to Peterson because he figured it out. Where is he? Did you kill him?"

"So many questions," he said, punctuating each word by digging his nails in. "It's time to go, Laney." He picked up her ankles, in spite of her flailing feet, and shoved her so far out the window that she tumbled head-first into the cold night air. Her scream was cut off as the hood of her jacket caught on the crooked shutter and her downward progress was halted for one precious moment. It gave her a millisecond to grab the shutter with her fingertips and cling there, legs scrabbling for purchase on the wood siding. Hardly daring to breath, she hung on with all her might, listening to the wood groaning under the stress. The ladder was a few tantalizing inches away. Salvation, if she could reach it.

Ancho poked a bat out of the window and used it to push the ladder away from the side. It fell with a soft plop on the snow below.

"Bye, honey," he said. "Try not to fall headfirst."

She started screaming even before he'd cleared the room. Peterson's house was so far away from the others she knew Ancho was right—no one was going to hear. *Max, Max,* her mind shrieked.

Fingers straining, she heard the sound of a motor as Ancho drove away, knowing she'd drop very soon. She pressed her feet against the wood to ease the load on her hands, but even so her joints were shaking with the effort of holding her there. She knew the old shutter would give way anytime.

Just to the other side of her she saw a downspout, sparkling with ice crystals. If she moved, she might break her grip and fall. If she didn't take some kind of action, she would undoubtedly plunge to the ground.

After as deep a breath as she could manage, she kicked out one leg. It banged against the downspout and fell uselessly away, nearly breaking her grip on the sill.

Come on, Laney. Focus.

This time, she aimed better and succeeded in getting her knee around the metal tube. There was a crooked part where it came away from the roof. It would be the only place for her to hang on, but it would mean she'd have to let go with one hand.

One shot and one shot only.

Just like short track, where one moment was all a skater was given to make her move, one moment that was the difference between triumph and disaster.

Sweat stung her eyes but she did not dare risk wiping it away. Muscles tensed, she put the fear aside and let go of the shutter with her left hand, grabbing desperately for the drain pipe.

She got hold of the crooked part and

wrapped her arm around it as tightly as she could before letting go with the other. A surge of triumph coursed through her as she fastened herself to the safety of the downspout.

Until she heard the soft groan of the metal as it began to detach itself from the wood siding.

NINETEEN

Some part of Max's subconscious told him to open his eyes and get up, but the pain in his midsection demanded he stay curled in a ball, squeezing air in and out of his lungs. It hurt to breathe, pained him to think and he got the sense he had passed out. It came back in a rush.

Laney. Ancho's here and he's going after Laney. The thought finally penetrated his fog and he forced himself to his knees, blinking against the spinning of the room. Levering himself upright using the table leg for support, he made it to his feet, stopping when a wave of dizziness nearly took him down. Staggering up the stairs, he tried to call her name, which came out as a gasp. He took the stairs as fast as he could manage until he burst, stumbling, into the bedroom.

"Laney," he grunted.

He was about to turn around and head back down the stairs when he heard a clang from outside the window. His stomach dropped. Thrusting his head through, he found her, clinging to a gutter of some sort that was about to detach from the wall.

In spite of the pain in his ribs, he shot out a hand, which she grabbed.

At that moment the metal twisted away from the building, carrying Laney with it, except for the anchor of their clasped hands.

She cried out in terror, eyes wide, mouth open.

He clung to her with all his strength, but her dead weight and the unfriendly angle made her hard to hold on to.

He grabbed her wrist with the other hand, trying to brace his legs against the wall but it would not hold, not for long. He had to pull her in but he could not manage the thing.

"Laney," he gasped. *Laney, don't leave me.* He felt her wrist begin to slip out of his grasp. "No," he grated, tightening his grip using some deep reserve of strength.

It was not enough. He heard her sharp intake of breath as she realized she was going to fall. *No, no. He could not let the most precious thing in his life slip away.*

And then there was a shout from below, a scraping sound and he saw the ladder being hoisted up against the wall. Just in time, Laney's feet found purchase on the metal rungs and there was a blessed release as he let go of her and watched her climb down the ladder to safety.

His body sagged in the window frame and all he could manage was to breathe in the cold air, to thank God Almighty for saving Laney from that fall. Exhausted, he let the pain carry him back to the floor, where he leaned there, panting.

Feet thundered up the steps and Laney burst in, running full tilt until she slid to her knees and reached for him, stopping before her hands actually touched his face.

"How badly are you hurt?" she said, expression torn with agony.

"Shouldn't I be asking you that?" he said.

The response must have reassured her because she pressed his face to hers, her lips brushing his cheek, then pressed to his mouth. "I thought he killed you."

Her pulse jumped so hard in her throat he could feel it thrumming, and he let himself fall into the comfort of that steady beating. Laney was all right. Unharmed. The pain in his own body seemed inconsequential. He'd been given the strength to hang on until help arrived and he knew it was not just his own strength that sustained them. An odd feeling of peace rang through his soul. He let her gently smooth her fingers over his arms and legs.

"Nothing broken?"

"Not unless it's a couple of ribs. I took a bat to the middle."

She gasped and her eyes filled. "Oh, Max. I'm so sorry about all of this. We'll get you to the hospital. You might have a punctured lung or something."

"Later, Laney. Who moved the ladder?" he managed as he arduously got to his feet with her help.

"That would be me," Tanya said from the doorway. "I came to see Mr. Peterson and, boy, was I surprised to see Laney hanging from the side of the house."

"I was surprised to find myself there, believe me," Laney said with a wobbly chuckle. She helped Max to a chair. "Ancho confirmed it. He's afraid I'll remember who was driving the car that night. That's why he's trying to get me out of competition. The longer I'm in, the better my chance of remembering."

Tanya's face blanched. "This is about what happened back then? That hit-and-run."

"I think so," Laney said. "If I could just remember who was in the driver's seat, this whole thing would be over."

Max's reasoning skills seemed to be returning. "Tanya, what did you want to tell Peterson? Why did you come here?"

"And how?" Laney added. "You don't have a car."

"I hitchhiked."

Both Laney and Max fired disapproving looks at her.

She fisted her hands on her hips. "Yeah, I know. Dangerous, but at least people aren't hitting me with bats and dropping me out of windows." She flopped on the bed. "After the accident, Mr. Peterson came to ask me questions, said he was a reporter and what did I know about a white car and who might have been driving it. I told him I had no idea. We were pretty focused on making the team at that point, and massively disappointed when we didn't. Anyway, I didn't think much about it until he showed up at the arena to talk to you a few days ago. Again he gave me his card and said if I had remembered any pertinent details to let him know."

"And did you remember something important?" Laney said, sitting next to her on the brown coverlet.

"I'm not sure." Tanya twisted at a thin silver band on her pinky. "I don't want to get anyone in trouble."

Max sat as straight as he could manage. "We're not trying to cause trouble, and we won't spread around unfounded accusations."

Tanya didn't answer.

"Tanya," he said softly. "Laney could have been badly hurt, and she's already been knocked out of the trials one time. Don't you think she deserves a little help if you can give it?"

Tanya sighed. "You're the nicest person on our team, Laney. And you've been sweet to me even though I haven't gone out of my way to be your friend. Anyway," she continued, fingers plucking at the blanket, "when I saw that you had my sharpening kit, the whole thing came back to me. After the trials, I was on my way home and I realized I'd left my kit in the locker room. I called Beth and asked her to get it for me." She frowned. "She didn't sound right."

"What do you mean?"

"She was distant, I guess. Slow. Not her usual sassy self. I figured it was because she hadn't qualified and everyone had been so sure she would. Even her mother believed she was going to make it. Beth was expecting a big gift or something. Anyway, I thought that's why she was acting funny."

"Did she agree to get the kit?" Max pressed.

"Yeah. She said she'd grab it before she left, but when I talked to her a couple of days later, she said she'd forgotten to go back to the locker room. I called the arena, but they'd hadn't found it there, either." Tanya frowned. "I got mad because Beth was so cavalier about it. She's got plenty of her mother's money to throw around, but that kit was a gift from my grandmother and it's not like she can round up the cash to buy another one at the drop of a hat."

"So you came to tell Peterson because you heard we'd found it in an abandoned white car."

She nodded. "Yes, but I was going to tell him that it wasn't anything to do with Beth. I'm sure she wasn't the driver. She drives a green Miata and she didn't even have it there at the trials. Besides, she'd never want to hurt you, Laney. She's snotty and spoiled, but inside she's a good person."

"But someone does want to hurt me. It wasn't Ancho who bent my skate."

Tanya looked away.

"Tanya," Max said quietly. "Do you have some idea who tampered with Laney's skates?"

"I thought I saw…" She stood. "No. No, I don't. I just wanted to tell Mr. Peterson about the kit because maybe it might help find out who hit you, but that's all I know. It wasn't Beth, so maybe someone else took my kit, some stranger who was watching the races. This man who just tried to shove you out the window, maybe."

"Maybe," Laney said. "But Peterson seems to think Ancho is covering for someone else, and I have this sense it was a woman driving the car that night. Are you sure you don't know who messed with my blade?"

Tanya's lips thinned into a firm line. "I've said all I'm going to."

Laney's phone buzzed and she snatched it up. "It's a text from Peterson. 'Had to get out fast. Contact you soon. H.P.'" She blew out a breath. "Thank goodness. I thought Ancho might have killed him or something."

"Wish we had gotten that text earlier," Max said with a groan. "It would have saved us all some pain."

"Should we call the police?" Laney said.

"It would be the right thing to do," Max said.

"But Chen already doesn't believe us, and we let ourselves into Peterson's house," Laney said.

Anger flashed in his gut. "Ancho should not get away with attacking either one of us."

"I know," Laney said, eyes shifting in thought. "But I think we should wait until we hear from Peterson. Maybe he has something the police will believe."

Max wasn't at all sure it was the right decision, but the searing pain in his ribs made it hard to argue. Each breath was a small agony. With some effort he closed the window, and they did the same for the sliding door as they left.

Tanya, he noticed, avoided eye contact as they drove. She knew something about who tampered with the blade, and her reluctance to speak confirmed for him that it was a person deeply connected with the team.

Maybe even Tanya herself.

Laney insisted Max have an X-ray at the hospital after they dropped Tanya back at the dorms. While he grudgingly allowed a nurse to lead him away, she went to see Jen and found there had been some improvement in her father's vital signs, the only high note in a disastrous evening. She gave Jen a gentle version of the night's events that did not include her hanging from a windowsill.

"This is getting dangerous," Jen said. "You've got to go to the police."

"As soon as we hear from Peterson," Laney said as she took her post beside the bed. "I want you to go sleep in my room at the athlete dorms tonight."

"Isn't that against the rules?"

"No one will mind for one night. We can get you a hotel tomorrow. Cubby needs the company. He likes a little warm milk before bed."

"Okay, I'll stay there only until morning to provide room service for Cubby. Your training starts at seven, right?" her sister inquired. "I'm sure Max will bring me here when he picks you up."

"Yes, I will," said Max from the doorway. "If that's what Laney wants."

Laney's heart ached at the sight of him, standing slightly hunched against the pain in his ribs, a bruise on his cheek, the magnificent blue eyes dulled by the hospital lighting. She didn't want to disappoint him, and she didn't want to have him walk out of her life, but her decision whether or not to continue could not be about Max Blanco. That was a choice between Laney and God.

"I'll pray on it, and by the morning I'll let you know." She came close. "Anything broken?"

"Two cracked ribs. They taped me up."

"Can they do anything for the pain?"

He gave her a roguish smile. "Pain? What pain?"

"Oh, boy. You're starting to sound like the old Blaze Blanco." She bit her lip, wondering if she had hurt him with the remark.

He reached out a hand and stroked her hair. "I think I'm better than Blaze Blanco. He was too interested in winning to notice what he was losing."

She hugged him very gently, a storm of emotions rolling through her. "Thank you for not letting me fall."

A sigh ruffled her hair. "That's my job."

His job. She felt him step away, and her arms mourned the loss. "If you train tomorrow, that will give you two more working days until the trials and a day to rest. You can still make it happen. I'll wait to hear from you."

Why did her heart feel as if it were being tugged and twisted in her chest? Everything that had been so certain only days before was now shrouded in confusion. "Yes," she managed.

"Try to get some sleep," her sister said, kissing her cheek.

"I will," Laney said, watching until they disappeared into the dark corridor.

She circled back to her father's bedside and smoothed his sheets before settling into the chair. Chin resting on the bed rail, she began to talk to her father, to tell him everything that had happened, all the fears, hopes and terrors that raced around inside her faster than any skater could lap the track.

But she could not say the one fear that plucked at her deepest core, the fear that Max Blanco had become much more to her than just a trainer, and soon, race or not, he would walk out of her life. That fear she gave to God, closing her eyes and pouring out all that she was and all that she wanted to be before Him.

TWENTY

The pain in his ribs forced Max out of bed long before the sun rose. He eased his body into the shower and then into workout clothes, propelling himself into the cold. He hoped it would numb the discomfort. It didn't.

As he limped through a slow walk, thoughts churned in frothy confusion through his mind. If Peterson didn't come through soon, they would go to the police regardless, and Laney would likely leave the team if Ancho decided to sue them for slander. He desperately did not want her to lose her shot that way, to have it taken from her like his had been. He knew she'd be fine; she was strong and she knew who she was made to be.

Who God made her to be.

The phrase tantalized him. What if all this

time that he'd been mourning the loss of his brother, his career, God had been using his pain to turn him into the man he was meant to be?

But who was that?

He wasn't sure, but just thinking about it warmed a spot of hope in his heart that he had not felt in a very long time. He would not indulge thoughts of the future now, though. His focus had to be on Laney, keeping her safe, helping her win if that was what she wanted and then letting her go. The thought made his heart break a little, and he knew he'd let himself skate dangerously close to loving Laney Thompson. Too close.

Four laps around of brisk walking and he had to stop, hands pressed to his side. Jen found him there. He looked at her. She was bundled up as if she was expecting a blizzard.

"Heard from Laney?" she said.

"No. You?"

She shook her head. "She's not a quitter, Max."

"I know, but she loves you and her father more than racing." His stomach was tight as he walked her to the truck. He noticed Jen had a set of books tucked under one arm. "Getting some studying in?"

"Trying to prep for the next semester classes. Genetics two. I nearly crumbled in genetics one."

"You put much stock in it? Genetics, I mean?"

"Some. Things we get from our birth parents—eye color, hair color, stature." She laughed. "Even certain types of sneezing."

"Now you're pulling my leg."

"Honest. The Achoo Syndrome. Uncontrollable sneezing when exposed to sudden changes in light."

He laughed heartily. "And they call this science." He wiped his eyes. "I've always believed you could make your body into what you wanted it to be. That's my job, I guess. It was a blow to my pride when I found I couldn't make it happen no matter how hard I tried."

"Yeah, that's the frustrating part." She nodded. "You get a certain stack of ingredients and that's genetics, your gifts from God, so to speak. How you stir them all together and use them is your gift to Him."

He opened the truck door for her. "How did you and your sister get so smart, I wonder?"

"Dunno, but my sister is definitely one of those gifts from God."

Memories of Robby stirred in his soul just then. Popsicles dripping in sticky hands on a summer evening. A fishing trip where he'd shown his brother how to bait a hook. Even though they'd only caught a sodden glove, it was the best fishing trip he'd ever taken.

He realized he was staring into space.

"You okay?" she asked quietly.

"Yes," he said. "I was just thinking about my brother."

"Laney told me he died when he was small. I'm sorry."

"Me, too," Max said.

"He was a gift from God," she said, her voice almost a whisper.

"Yes, he was."

They arrived at the hospital where Max was surprised to find Stan and Jackie standing awkwardly in Dan's room. No sign of Laney.

"We thought we'd come and give our good wishes," Stan said. "The nurse gave us special permission to come in before visiting hours."

Jackie shrugged, sliding a plant covered with coral blooms onto the shelf next to the heart monitor. "He hasn't woken up."

They made small talk for a few minutes until Stan checked his watch. "We'd better go. We have to prep for training today. Ice time in less than an hour." He shot Max a questioning look.

"I have to talk to Laney," Max said. "I don't know what she wants to do."

"She has to decide," Jackie said. "One hundred percent."

Max stiffened. "I'm aware of that."

Laney appeared in the doorway, her hair in disarray and eyes smudged with fatigue, but something shone in her face, wild and strong, which made his pulse accelerate.

"What's going on, Laney?"

"I remembered."

He stared. "Remembered?"

"Something about the accident." She strode

farther into the room. "There were two people in that white car."

Jen gasped. "Two? Can you remember their faces?"

"Not yet, but I will," she snapped. "I always imagined it was one driver, someone drunk or really young who panicked and left us there, but there were two people. One could have gone for help. They no doubt talked about what to do and…"

"And they left us," Max said, a slow burn starting in his gut that matched the kindling in her eyes.

"Yes, they did. And one more thing about the white car."

He held his breath and waited.

"There was something funny about the plates."

"Out of state?" Jen suggested.

"I don't know. It will come to me, but they weren't regular Utah plates."

Max wanted to catch her up in a big hug. "Good girl. That's enough to take to the police. Maybe it will help."

"Not yet."

"Why not?" Jackie said.

"Because we'll be late for training."

Max felt his spirit swell. "You ready to give it a try?"

"No," she said, gaze steady and calm but filled with steel. "I'm ready to win."

Laney attacked her workout with such vigor, the other girls gaped.

"What did you have for breakfast?" Tanya asked as they finished their sprints on the track.

"Nothing unusual." She dropped her voice so the other girls would not hear. "Did you give any more thought to who tampered with my skate?"

Tanya bent over, presumably to catch her breath. "No."

"I'm starting to remember things about the accident. I'm going to find out who crashed into us and left us there."

Tanya stopped. Her cheeks were so flushed it nearly concealed her spangle of freckles. "I hope you do, and I hope you can prove it."

Laney watched her walk away. Would her resurfacing memories be enough to prove anything? She noticed a man at the far end of the track wearing sunglasses and a pulled-down cap. Ancho? Her stomach clenched until she realized it was Hugh Peterson slouched at the edge of the track, hands shoved into his pockets.

She walked slowly over, and Max joined her. He hadn't taken his eyes off her the entire morning.

"We got attacked at your house," Max said, by way of greeting.

"No one told you to go in," Peterson said. "Saw Ancho's car come up the drive. I grabbed my papers and had time to get upstairs before he picked the lock and got in. I climbed out the window. You must have come along just after that."

"Unfortunately," Laney said. "What did you find out?"

"Someone we know and love happens to drive an Aston Martin."

"Who?"

"Me," Diane Morrison interjected, causing Laney to jump. None of them had noticed that she'd come up behind them. Beth stood next to her, hands folded across her chest.

Peterson flinched. "Yes, you, Mrs. Morrison. And you were also in town two weeks ago, and during that stay you visited Trevor Ancho."

Diane stared at them, eyes sparking. "Of course I did. We've been friends for a long time."

Beth nodded. "True. They went to college together, didn't you, Mom?"

"Sure. And the answer to your next question is Salt Lake City. That's where the Aston is. After I left here I drove it home and no, Trevor did not drive it anywhere because nobody operates that car except me."

Out of the corner of her eye, Laney noticed a security guard approaching with Jackie following close beside.

"So it's my turn now," Diane said, noting the guard's approach. "Before you get tossed out of here for sneaking into a closed practice. What gives you the right to pry into my life? Are you accusing me of something?"

"Could be," he said.

She broke into a hard smile. "Excellent, because as my daughter and my three ex-husbands will tell you, there's nothing I like more than a fight. If you are leveling an accusation, you'd better be absolutely sure about it because I have lawyers that will eat you for lunch, and I will watch every moment with complete enjoyment. Now, is there something else you wanted to know?"

"Just one more thing," Peterson said quietly. "This question is for Beth."

"Leave her out of it," Diane snapped.

"Sir," the guard said, reaching the bottom of the steps. "You don't have authorization to be in the arena right now."

Peterson leaned close. "What did Mommy give you for your sixteenth birthday?"

Beth's mouth opened then closed.

"I'm going to have to escort you out, sir." The guard took hold of Peterson's arm. As he was led away, his gaze remained fixed on Beth.

She stared back, mouth open, cheeks flushed.

Diane took her wrist. "He's a crackpot, kiddo. Put him out of your mind. Go suit up for ice work. Isn't that what's next, Jackie?"

Jackie nodded and ushered Beth back toward the locker rooms.

Diane glared at Max and Laney. "If Peterson's private-eye shtick is some ploy of yours to distract Beth from her training, it's not going to work."

Laney stiffened. "As Beth told me, there are ten spots on that team, and on race day they can belong to any one of us."

"To be perfectly honest, I don't care who wins or loses except that Beth is going to be one of the winners and no accusations or muckraking is going to change that." Diane lowered her voice. "I will bury anybody who gets in her way."

"Is that a threat, Diane?" A muscle in Max's jaw throbbed. "Like maybe you cooked up a plan with Ancho to scare Laney into quitting?"

"I don't have to beat Laney outside the rink, Max, because Beth will take care of that on the ice."

"We'll see," he said.

"Yes," she murmured, a confident smile on her lips. "We will."

Ice drills dragged for the first time in Max's experience. Normally he relished each and every moment, and the practice was finished long before he'd like it to be. Now he couldn't wait to get Laney through her practice so they could go somewhere safe and contact Peterson again. Finally she emerged from the changing room, hair wet from the shower.

"Tired?"

"Ready to drop," she affirmed. "Let's sit a minute."

After collapsing on a bench outside the arena, she called the hospital and was given an update. She put it on speakerphone so Max could hear. No change, and Jen had secured a hotel room five minutes from the hospital and rented a car. "I'm going to get a couple of hours of sleep before I shower and come back."

"It's my turn to spend the night," Laney started.

"In my medical opinion, people who train hard all day need to have a minimum of six hours in their beds, not sprawled on a hospital chair."

"I concur," Max put in.

Laney sighed. "Okay, but I'm going to

come visit before lights out if I can force my body to stay awake."

"How'd training go?"

Laney shot a look at Max. "Interesting. We may have gotten some further helpful information from Peterson." She promised to keep her sister apprised and clicked off.

Max was staring at the mountains, which were painted in deep purple by the waning sun. "So Peterson figured out a connection between Diane and Ancho. Let's say she's lying and she convinced Ancho to loan money to Dan and put the muscle on him. She let Ancho borrow the Aston Martin for some reason. He goes nuts and sticks you in the trunk, then hides the car away so you can't pin it on him. It still doesn't prove she was involved in the accident four years ago."

"She wasn't even in town during the trials, that I'm aware of, but maybe she hired Ancho to cover up for the driver."

Max knew she didn't want to say it aloud so he did it for her. "Beth."

Laney shook her head. "No, it couldn't be true. Beth would not leave me there."

"She was young. She panicked. Called her

mom, who arranged for Ancho to make the white car disappear."

"Oh, no," Laney said. "That's what Peterson was getting at. Tanya told me that Diane had planned a big present to celebrate Beth's birthday. You don't suppose she bought her..."

"A white car."

"Oh, Max," Laney said, tears gathering in her eyes. "That's what I remembered. The strange plates. They were the kind they put on new cars until you get the real ones."

He took her hand. "I'll call Officer Chen," Max said. He expected an argument from Laney, but he didn't get one.

"I can't believe it's true," she whispered. "How could Beth leave us there?"

"Because her mom told her to," he said, squeezing her fingers.

He listened a moment, then left a message on Chen's voicemail about an urgent matter that needed a return call.

"Come on. You need to eat something, and then I'll take you to see your dad."

She stood and the tears let loose. He gathered her into his arms and rocked her back and forth, pressing a brief kiss to her mouth, wishing he could funnel all the tenderness that swirled inside him into her aching heart. "I'm sorry, Laney, but it's time for the truth to come out."

She returned the kiss tentatively, then with a sense of need that took his breath away. Warm cascades of tenderness that he had never felt for any other woman flooded his body, mind and soul. Finally she pressed her face to his chest as if she could keep the world away for one more moment. Then she straightened, wiped her face and put on the expression he'd seen so many times.

Go time.

Dan was partially awake, and alert enough to give Laney a smile, which seemed to infuse her with new vigor. As they returned to the truck, Officer Chen met them and insisted they go back inside the lobby to talk. Settled into green-covered chairs, screened from the quiet hallways by a massive potted tree, Max explained every detail, starting from their ill-advised visit to Peterson's house and ending with their trackside confrontation with Diane.

Chen listened in perfect stillness. "I can check out the Aston registration and whether or not Diane Morrison purchased a white car in the past four years, but until you can put a person behind the wheel, it isn't enough."

"What will be enough?" Max nearly shouted. "When Ancho kills Laney to keep her from placing Beth behind the wheel?"

"Please don't raise your voice. I can check out these leads, and we can start to ask questions, to reopen the case, but it would help if Laney could remember what happened that night."

Her eyes went wide. "I've tried so hard. It's all starting to come back faster and faster. I'm going to remember it all. Soon."

"The sooner the better."

Max saw that there was something underneath the carefully neutral expression on Chen's face. "You believe us, don't you?"

"I'm beginning to."

Finally. "Why?" Max said.

"Because Hugh Peterson was killed an hour ago."

TWENTY-ONE

Laney kept repeating the phrase over and over after Chen dismissed them with the promise to conduct a complete investigation.

Because Hugh Peterson was killed an hour ago.

How could that crabby, full-of-fire man be gone? His life had apparently ended when his car had slipped off the road and landed in a snow-clogged ravine ten miles from his house.

Max held her close in the hallway outside her room. "It was no accident," she breathed. "Ancho must have been watching, waiting for him to head back home."

"Or Diane called Ancho from the arena."

Laney's insides went cold. "How could anyone end a life like that? Why? To cover for Beth? I don't see why Ancho would do it."

"Because he's connected with Diane somehow. Maybe he loves her or has a debt to repay." Max rubbed her shoulders. "More than anything I think he just flat-out likes it. He enjoys the fact that he's got the town hoodwinked about what kind of person he really is."

"What's going to happen, Max?" she said, pulling away so she could look into his face.

"Ancho and Diane are going to know pretty quick that the police are poking around. I'm sure they'll both be questioned. They'd be fools to try anything else."

"What can I do? I feel responsible. Peterson got into this to find out the truth about our accident."

"That's for the police to ferret out. We're not putting ourselves in any more dangerous situations. All you need to do is focus on racing and your father's recovery."

She wanted to insert herself back into his embrace, to feel his strong arms around her that kept the bad things away, but he had already reached for the doorknob. "Keep your door locked and don't leave your room until I come and get you in the morning. I've talked to security and they are doubling their patrols at night until things are resolved. Outer doors are all locked. Let me come in and check your room just to ease my own mind."

The room was the same way she'd left it. Cubby mewled his displeasure at her tardiness, and she picked him up, talking sweetly into his ear until he squirmed to be put down. Max checked the bathroom and made sure the window was locked. He returned, staring at her with strange intensity.

"Max, you don't really think Ancho would come here, do you?"

"I absolutely do." He came close, putting his hands on her shoulders and looking as though he was going to kiss her again. She found herself yearning for him to do so, and her pulse fluttered for a moment until he stepped away. "Stay safe, Laney. You've got a race to run."

"No, I've got a race to win," she corrected.

He smiled, and she almost believed in that moment that that there could be a future in those blue eyes, the tired face, the wounded spirit that had carried such a burden for so many years.

"You have the heart of a lion," he said. "Maybe if I'd had…"

"Had what?"

He looked down. "I've been thinking I gave up too soon. Let myself get hardened inside and rooted in what I've lost."

She held her breath, not wanting to break the fragile thread of connection. "I know it was not easy for you to make me that little paper dinosaur. It brought back the grief you felt for your brother, and I know you did it for me."

He sighed. "I would do anything for you," he said, looking at her with such intensity his eyes blazed. "And that means coaching you to the finish line."

Something in the words saddened her. Was it still about that finish line? "What will you do, Max? After I get there, I mean."

They both knew if she did earn a slot, most of her coaching and training would be taken over by the U.S. team staff.

"One thing at a time, Laney, but you know wherever you're training, I'll be your biggest fan, even when I'm not there with you."

She nodded, unable to trust herself with words. *Even when I'm not there with you.*

He wished her good-night and waited outside in the hallway until she slid the bolt home.

The finish line. She felt as if she was closer than she'd ever been, but it would require an incredible effort to keep away thoughts of her father, Ancho and Diane. She prayed for a while, checked in with Jen and then listened to music on her iPod. At long last she put on her sweats and lay down. The morning would come soon enough. Somehow things never seemed as dire when the sun was shining. Still, she was glad for her night-light, which spread a tiny comforting glow in the darkness.

She was startled awake later. Had it been an hour? A few minutes? She was not sure. Blinking, she sat up trying to identify what had happened. It was three o'clock in the morning, her little travel clock told her. Her phone showed no evidence of a text or email. Bad dream? Possibly, but she could not remember what it might have been about.

Trying to force her brain to picture the driver of the white car had not helped at all. The memory remained stubbornly sequestered. It simply could not be Beth, not the girl she'd known for years, her teammate and compatriot. Sure, Beth was catty and man crazy, but she'd also offered to get Laney a new trainer and loan her some skates.

Laney got up and checked the door. Still locked. Chiding herself for paranoia, she went to the tiny dorm-size refrigerator and helped herself to orange juice. As she raised the cup to her lips, a shadow reflected off the glass and she realized with a flash of horror that she was not alone.

When his phone buzzed, Max put down the Winston Churchill biography he'd spent the past four hours trying to read. Part of him hoped it was a sleepless Laney so he could reassure himself with the sound of her voice. The other part, the trainer's part, wanted her to be getting a solid seven hours before the last day of serious training was to start.

"Max, it's Tanya."

He straightened. "Are you all right?"

"Sure."

He waited, but she did not continue. "It's pretty late."

"I know, but I heard what happened to Mr. Peterson and I can't get it out of my mind. I think I should tell you about the skates." Her voice dropped to a whisper. "I don't want to be overheard talking or I'll be in trouble for breaking curfew. Can you meet me at the bridge?"

He should advise her against going out after curfew, but he had a profound sense that he needed to hear what she had to say. Immediately.

"On my way. Keep talking to me as we walk so I can make sure you're safe."

Her hurried breaths indicated she was nervous, the squeak of what he assumed to be the door sounded softly as she let herself out. He made out her figure slipping through the night and in a few minutes she was there.

"Go ahead, I'm listening."

She sucked in a deep breath and hunched into the jacket she'd thrown over her pajamas.

"That day, right before we raced, I thought I saw…"

Seconds ticked by. "Tell me, Tanya, it's important."

"I thought I saw someone messing around in Laney's gear, but it was dark and I might have been mistaken."

"Who?"

"What if I'm wrong, Max? I could ruin a reputation and get myself involved with untrue accusations. My own skating career might be over."

He forced a breath in and out, keeping his tone level by sheer will. "Please, Tanya. Hugh Peterson is dead and Laney might be next."

There was a long pause.

"I saw Jackie Brewster with her hand in Laney's bag."

Disbelief dumbed his senses as the name circled thickly in his mind. "Jackie? Why would she do that?"

"I don't know. That's why I figured I must have been mistaken." Tanya chewed her lip. "Why would Beth's coach mess with Laney's skates?"

Because she was covering for her athlete, the girl she'd allowed to leave the scene of the accident. Beth had driven away and Jackie knew it.

"She grabbed the skate after the race and hid it. Later she gave it to Ancho to get rid of, and I stopped him before he tossed it in the lake."

Tanya's face shone white in the darkness. "She could have killed Laney by messing with her skates, or another racer if she spun out of control."

Max's stomach dropped to the snow. Or she could be going after an unaware Laney right now.

He grabbed his phone and dialed Laney's number. If she read him the riot act for awakening her, it would be balm to his ears. The phone went to voicemail. Perhaps she was sound asleep and didn't hear it. With her father in the hospital? He knew she'd be sleeping with the phone nearby. He took off at a hard sprint, heedless of Tanya, who gave a cry of surprise as he bolted past her.

Laney. Her sweet smile filled his consciousness. She would let Jackie in, of course, because she refused to see the worst in people. It was something very precious and God breathed, but at that moment it might condemn her to death. He could see the curtained window of her room, second from the end of the hallway. No light showed through the heavy fabric.

He pounded up the walkway, fumbling for his pass key. A hand reached out and stopped him.

"Problem, sir?" the security guard asked.

"I've got to get in," Max panted. "There could be someone after Laney Thompson."

He pulled out his phone. "Do you have her number? I'll call her."

"I tried that. She's not answering."

"All right." The man spoke soothingly. "I'll go in and knock on her door. Which one is it?"

"Listen," Max said, his voice hard and loud. "I'm her trainer, and I'm going in there, and you're gonna get out of my way."

The man was big, muscular and almost as tall as Max. "I don't think that's a good idea, sir. We were told no one was to have admittance after-hours to the woman's dorm, no exceptions."

Okay, he thought to himself. He used to be a man who didn't let anything get between himself and the finish line. He'd thought that man was gone.

Time to think again.

Laney whirled around, but she was too slow. Hands caught her from behind, and a piece of thick tape was slapped over her mouth. She kicked, but the person behind her swept her legs out from under her and she found herself on her back on the bed. More tape was applied to her hands.

Someone turned on the small lamp next to her bed and Laney gasped as Ancho's face swam in front of her.

She tried to jerk to her feet, but he stepped forward and threw her back on the bed. Laney had been scared plenty of times in her life, but nothing compared to the knife edge of fear that cut at her insides.

Ancho calmly opened a Ziploc bag of cookies and put them on the bedside table. Cookies? Was he crazy?

Ancho's mouth quirked cruelly in the dim light. "Killed by a cookie. I love it." Ancho held the cookie up to Laney's face and the fear crystallized on the pungent smell of peanuts.

"You didn't realize they had peanuts when you took them to your room," Ancho whispered, almost soothingly. "Stupid girl. You had an allergic reaction."

No, no, no.

He peeled back a corner of the tape and pressed the cookie to Laney's mouth. Laney jerked her head away, lips rammed together.

"Oh, quit playing around," Ancho said, grabbing Laney's head and holding it still while he forced the bite inside her mouth. She fought hard not to swallow, but Ancho pressed his hand over Laney's mouth and nose until she was forced to suck in a breath and with it, the cookie. Coughing and choking, she bucked against Ancho's hold.

There was a sound of the door opening. Someone to rescue her.

Jackie Brewster appeared at the bedside, eyes rounded in horror. "This is not right," she hissed. "You were supposed to scare her, that's all." She plucked at his hands, but he shoved her away. "You were supposed to make the car disappear. That's what Diane paid you to do."

"I did. Didn't know the kid found the sharpening kit. And it's not my fault that skater girl here started to remember everything. I went above and beyond trying to persuade her to quit by putting the screws to her father and taking her for a ride in the Aston."

Laney's thoughts reeled. Jackie knew? The flash of memory nearly blinded her. The two people in the car. Beth behind the wheel and in the passenger seat... Jackie Brewster.

Jackie's eyes darted helplessly, her voice a whisper. "I'm sorry. I really am. I never should have given Beth a sedative, but she was distraught. She ran out, got into that ridiculous car her mother had delivered for her birthday and crashed."

Into us. And she left us. And you let her.

"I called Diane. She told us to drive it to his place." Jackie gave Ancho a disgusted look.

"Too much jabbering," Ancho snapped.

"This is not right," Jackie said, reaching

for the phone. "I won't let you murder her. It's gone too far."

He dealt her a cruel blow to the back of the head that crumpled her to the floor, her hand still outstretched toward the phone as she fell.

No help. No rescue.

Laney forced herself into a calmer zone. Her only way to save herself now was strategy. Sense the weakness and take advantage of it, Max would say. She felt a longing overwhelm every pore, a deeply rooted need to see Max again, to laugh and live and celebrate life with him for as many days as God would give them. Fighting against every instinct, she forced her body to go still.

Ancho let go of her head, still crouched over her. He leaned down to peel the rest of the tape away, and that was when Laney made her move. With legs made of iron from hour upon hour of practice, she kicked out harder than any start she'd ever made. Her feet exploded into Ancho, knocking him over backward.

Still, he managed to get to his feet and cut off her escape path to the door.

Her throat felt itchy and her tongue thick and useless. She gasped for breath.

Ancho laughed. "Cat got your tongue?"

She tried to yell, but all that came out was a wheezy grunt.

"I don't even need to lay a finger on you," he chuckled. "I'm just going to sit here and watch you die."

For what? she wanted to scream. *For some payoff from Diane? A favor you owed her?*

She decided then, her brain fogging over and eyes watering, that even if she lost, she would not let him win. Praying for a few more seconds, she picked up the chair. Ancho's eyes widened as he realized her intent. Before he could lunge for her, she swung the chair with all her might and sent it crashing through the window, sending a shower of glass into the cold winter air.

TWENTY-TWO

Max was getting ready to shove past the guard just as Laney's window exploded. He didn't waste any time in more conversation but, skirting the stunned guard, slammed his key into the lock and sprinted to Laney's room, the guard right behind him. He was in time to see a figure dashing down the darkened hallway toward the dining area.

"I'm on him," the guard said, going in pursuit.

Max barreled through Laney's door and his heart seized. She was facedown on the floor next to Jackie's crumpled form.

Tanya ran in. "What happened?"

"Turn on the lights," he shouted.

Tanya flipped the switch and he knelt next to Laney, frantically checking for bruises or blood. "I don't see anything. Call the medic. See if you can help Jackie."

Tanya did so while he put his cheek to her mouth. She was breathing, but it was a wheezy, high-pitched sound. Out of his peripheral vision, he saw the bag of cookies.

"Oh, no." He leaped to his feet. "Where's her EpiPen? Help me find it. It's in a yellow pack that she carries with her."

Tanya held the phone in one hand and dumped out Laney's purse. "It's not here."

Max saw the corner of Laney's training bag where it had been kicked under the desk. With fingers gone cold, he unzipped it and found the yellow box, tearing open the top and unwrapping the hypodermic.

Laney's face was a bluish color, eyes closed, lips swollen. *Please, God,* he prayed as he deployed the needle into her upper thigh. There was no reaction. He rolled her on her side to ease her breathing.

"When's the medic coming?" he shouted to Tanya.

"He's here," she said, as the man pushed by her.

"Ambulance is on its way," the medic said.

Fear and helplessness surged through Max as he clung to Laney's hand while the medic monitored her pulse and breathing and checked Jackie, whom he found to be breathing normally.

Please. He'd begged just the same way when Robby lay dying, and God had answered no. So many years the anger of that denial had shaped his life. Now he asked not with the child's faith, but the desperate hope of a wounded man who had lately begun to believe that the Father who denied him his brother had not abandoned Max Blanco.

"Laney," he said, voice breaking. "Stay with me. Please stay with me."

The security guard appeared in the doorway, panting heavily, holding a cuffed Ancho, who still held on to his arrogant grin. "Looks like she's gotten hold of some peanuts, poor thing."

Now a crowd of girls began to cluster in the darkened hallway.

"What is going on here?" came the authoritative voice of Coach Stan. The hallway was suddenly brilliantly illuminated.

Ancho sneezed violently multiple times.

A sizzling realization went through Max's brain. He remembered after the lake episode, someone else who'd had a violent sneezing fit when the lights were turned on. He looked at Ancho. Max wanted to say something vicious to this insane man who had conspired with Jackie to kill Laney, but there was no space in his thoughts for hatred, only worry for Laney, the woman his heart finally admitted he loved desperately.

The guard shoved Ancho toward the sound of the police sirens and paramedics crowded the tiny room, ordering them all out in no uncertain terms. Max reluctantly stepped to the hallway, where he nearly plowed into Beth.

He saw it there now, guilt buried deep in her eyes and he wondered why he had not noticed it before. "You hit us, that night. You hit us and you drove away."

Her face crumpled. "I didn't want to, but Jackie made me. I was groggy. I was upset."

Pity and disgust mixed together. "All these years you could have come forward, but you didn't. Your coach and your mother covered up for you and you let them."

"I tried to help Laney when I could," she whispered.

He took her shoulder and turned her to look through the doorway. "Look how you helped her, Beth."

Beth gasped at the sight of Laney with an oxygen mask being strapped to a stretcher while another was being rolled in for Jackie.

"They said if I told the truth, I'd never race again," she whispered, tears running down her face.

Ancho jerked to a stop before the guard propelled him out the far hallway door. "Don't tell them anything, baby."

"Baby?" Beth croaked.

"I think he's your father," Max said, and a hush fell over the hallway.

"My father?" Beth's face went slack with shock. "That's not true. I hardly even know him." She looked again at Laney. "I just wanted to win." She started to sob then, the uninhibited wails of a young girl. "I'm so sorry."

Her naked grief stirred him with pity. Of all the people involved in the accident, maybe Beth was more a victim of Jackie and her mother than Laney. He took Beth in his arms and hugged her. After a deep breath he said, "I know."

Three days later, Laney looked in his direction only once after she suited up and stepped into the hot box before the race, skin suit open a few inches at the neck, ear buds in place. It was okay, she was in the zone and he knew she carried a little piece of him with her; the little paper bird he'd cut out for her was pressed next to her heart.

This time, as he'd waited in the hospital corridor, knowing Laney would survive the anaphylactic episode unharmed, he cut the paper not with strokes of anger or fear, but with a profound sense of peace. Each snip brought some healing until the place inside that had been tattered was now fresh and clean, like the crisp white paper on which he worked.

Pale and teary eyed, she'd accepted that small offering, it seemed to him, with that same sense of peace in her face, shadowed perhaps by sadness at the betrayal by people she had trusted and cared about.

"I feel terrible about Beth," she'd said in a small voice.

"Me, too."

After a few moments of plucking at the hospital sheets, she'd heaved a sigh, tears trickling down her cheeks. "Thank you, Max, for everything."

No, thank you, he'd wanted to say. Thank you for that sweet spirit and gentle heart, the steady faith that cast light into his own life where it was desperately dark. Instead of talking, he'd clutched her hand and just watched her, drinking in the fact that she was safe and well and still in his life.

And now here she was, ready to race. The other girls did not mention the absence of both Beth and Jackie, though Coach Stan had briefed them all as tactfully as he could, sticking to the facts and quashing any speculation. He'd already been on the phone all morning, talking to the parents of the skaters or speaking to them in person as they arrived to watch their kids compete in the ultimate race. The bald truth was harsh. Beth's skating career was over, her legal future uncertain, and both Jackie and Diane Morrison were in custody, along with Trevor Ancho.

Jen patted him on the shoulder. "Dad's glued to the television, but he insisted I come and watch it live."

"I'm glad he's going to be okay."

"He'll have to make some lifestyle adjustments and go through therapy, but we'll manage." She regarded him slyly. "I heard you telling Laney that Ancho is Beth's father. And you thought I was pulling your leg about heredity."

He laughed. "Who would have thought Beth got that photosensitive sneezing from her father? I didn't figure it out until…" He did not want to cast his mind back to Laney's room, to remember her struggling for breath. "Anyway, it's just weird, but it further explains why he was willing to go to such lengths for her."

"Maybe Beth and her father have more in common than the Achoo Syndrome."

He sighed. Heredity really was a strange thing. Laney and Jen were biological products of a drug addict, yet because of the love of a man who had not fathered them and the grace of a Heavenly Father, they were both spectacular women.

He wondered what would become of Beth. "Sad thing is she didn't even know he was her father. Diane kept that from her, too, apparently."

They went quiet as the racers took their places at the start line. His pulse revved.

Focus on your race plan.

Plant the tip of your blade.

Explosive start.

The starting buzzer sounded and the racers surged forward. *Go time.*

Laney exploded from the start line with perfect form and laser-like concentration. Max experienced each turn, each straightaway as his heart beat with hers. The pack of skaters ebbed and flowed around her.

Every backbreaking practice, inhuman workout, the hours upon hours of mental preparation came to bear on that four-lap race. He knew she was going to win. Five hundred meters and forty seconds later, she did just that.

First place, with Tanya coming in second. Both snagged a place on the U.S. team.

When she crossed the finish line, arms raised in triumph, Laney looked for him.

He smiled, cheeks wet with tears, as Laney took her victory lap and he felt every inch of it, deep down in his soul. When she made it to the side of the ice, she reached up to him and they twined their arms together. Over the roar of the spectators, he kissed her. It wasn't a congratulatory kiss or even a gesture of the deep friendship they shared, but a kiss of love that shone in his heart brighter than burnished gold.

"I love you, Birdie," he breathed.

Her laughter was effervescent. "Love you back. Always and forever."

"Bend lower, back parallel to the ice," Max said. "Tuck your hands behind you when you get into the flow of it." The arena was empty now, no sign of the electric excitement that had infused the place the day before when Laney had won the five-hundred-and one-thousand-meter events to cement her spot on the U.S. team. She'd been immediately engulfed by the media, who had gotten wind of her story and the scandal that had inevitably surfaced when the arrests were made.

Nolan crouched down to the ice and Max skated closer and showed him how to position his arm and dig in for the start.

Nolan took off and made it several yards before he lost the proper form, put his head down and just flat-out skated hard and fast.

Max laughed.

The kid would be a good speed skater someday, maybe even a great one.

"Looks like he needs a trainer," Laney said, leaning against the rail.

"Hey there. You got away from the reporters and fans all clamoring for your time?"

She chuckled. "Now I know why stars sneak out the back exits. Actually, I've been with my dad, but I did get to tell him I've been signed by a sponsor. I thought it would help his recovery to know that."

"Absolutely."

"Coach Stan was named as head coach, in spite of the whole mess."

He nodded. "Excellent. You've got a great coach, the best facilities and a sponsor—everything you need to bring home a medal."

She ran a finger along the wood. "I wish you could continue to train me."

"You'll have the best in the world doing that."

Nolan zipped by, flashing them a cocky grin.

"Are you going to train Nolan?" she asked.

"No, but I'm going to make sure he takes advantage of your scholarship program and gets his skate in the door, so to speak. I've put a call in to his mother to discuss it with her."

"That's great. We never really talked about the future." She chewed her lip. "What are you going to do?"

Now that the victory flush of the race had died away, he felt less sure. Maybe he'd caught her in a breathtaking moment and the sentiment they'd shared in that instant didn't carry over. The silence lingered for a moment before he steadied his nerves. "I'm going to train."

"Who?"

He heaved out a breath. *Ready to make it real, Blanco?* "Me."

She blinked. "What?"

"I'm going to give it four years and try one more time to make the team."

Her gasp carried through the arena. "Max, that's great. Why did you change your mind?"

"All this time I've been racing angry, trying to beat the physical restrictions of my body because of the rage inside me." He paused and gathered up the words. "You made me see that I should have been racing because that's what I was made to do, for the joy of it. I'm going to try it one more time, for the right reasons, and see where it gets me. Maybe the Winter Games, maybe not, but I've got to find out."

She vaulted over the railing and wrapped him in a huge hug that sent him skidding a few paces and nearly knocked them both to the ice. She pressed kisses all over his face. "I'm so happy for you and I'm going to cheer you on every step of the way." She fisted her arms in the air. "Blaze is back!" she chortled.

He had to laugh at the enthusiasm. "I've got a long way to go before I'm back, but at least I'm ready to start."

When their laughter died away she tried to

let go, but he didn't allow it. Instead, he held her tight. "You know I love you."

She nodded.

"It's not the right time."

A frown pulled the corners of her mouth, and pain rippled through her eyes. "But…"

"You're going to be busy this year, training for that gold medal. You think I pushed you hard? Just wait until the U.S. team trainers get hold of you."

Her body felt so slight in his arms, the light gilding her hair with platinum.

"Yes," she agreed, head cocked. "But I can take it. I'm ferocious, some would say."

"I wondered…" He cleared his throat. "I've got something for you to keep with you, if you want it."

She smiled. "You know I am going to keep the little paper bird with me always."

"This is something that might go with the medal you're going to win. Another kind of gold." He took the slender band from his pocket.

Her eyes went wide. "Max?"

He looked into her sweet face, still brimming with a zeal for life in spite of the fire she'd been through, her faith polished and refined by the tragedies. "Laney, you're the greatest prize I could ever hope to win. I love you, I've always loved you and I always will." He stared in painful uncertainty as she looked at the engagement ring. Maybe it was too late, he'd started too slow and the race that truly mattered had gotten away from him.

"I didn't think you felt that way," she breathed, looking away from him. "You love me enough to marry me? Why?"

There were so many reasons, chapters and verses of them, all fighting to be first out of his mouth. He settled on only one. "When I'm with you, I'm a better man." How simple, how inadequate and how little he had to offer this woman who had her whole bright future ahead of her.

"Max Blanco," she said, looking him in the eye, "it's about time you realized that." She slid the ring onto her finger and beamed a smile more golden than pure sunlight. "I love you."

Sparks of joy exploded in his body as he pulled her close and kissed her, feeling that he'd finally gotten his life off the start line, heading in the perfect direction God had meant for him all along.

* * * * *

Dear Reader,

It's always a thrill to watch the Winter Games, don't you think? I remember watching Apolo Anton Ohno over the years as he won his eight medals and being fascinated by his testimony: a rebellious teenager who was raised by a single father who drove him to a remote cabin and left him there to sort out his priorities. Ohno did, and, with some divine inspiration, he became the world's most decorated winter athlete of all time. Athletes are an inspiration to all of us not because they skate fast or break records, but because of who they are and how God has led them to a place where their flame burns bright enough to light up the world.

As we take time out of our lives to watch the spectacle unfold before us, we can all stand in the glow of those amazing lives, touched by God and shared with the world. I'll be watching, will you?

I am so pleased that you took the time to read my book. It's always a joy to hear from readers via my website at www.danamentink.com. If you prefer to correspond via mail, there is a physical address posted on the website, as well. God bless.

Sincerely,

Dana Mentink

Questions for Discussion

1. Have you ever failed at a goal that others around you achieved? How did you handle the feelings that ensued?

2. Max and Laney are passionate about their sport. What hobbies or pursuits are you passionate about?

3. Some people accept disappointment with grace and others with bitterness. How does the Bible advise us to deal with disappointment?

4. Foster parents change children's lives. What qualities must a person have to tackle the role of foster parent?

5. Laney said, "What I do is skate fast. I'm not changing the world." Why does our culture worship athletic performances?

6. God offers different pursuits over the course of our lives. How is it possible to decide which pursuits to follow? Or when to give up a passion from our youth?

7. We all have the same number of minutes in the day. How can we make them count for something bigger than accomplishing day-to-day business?

8. Max's deepest fear was that he was truly alone. What comfort would you offer him?

9. Laney's father made a bad decision for a good reason. Have you ever done the same? What was the result?

10. Max was at a loss about how to comfort Laney when her father had a heart attack. What do you feel is the best way to help someone in such a difficult situation?

11. Fire refines gold as trials refine and purify our faith. Do you agree with this statement?

12. Which is stronger, the power of heredity or the power of love? Explain your thinking.

13. Max wondered if he'd been too interested in winning to notice what he'd been los-

ing. Do you think this was true? Are we as a society facing this problem, as well?

14. What do you think God made you to be? How do you know?

15. Will you be watching the Winter Games this year? What sport is your favorite and why?

REQUEST YOUR FREE BOOKS!
2 FREE RIVETING INSPIRATIONAL NOVELS IN TRUE LARGE PRINT PLUS 2 FREE MYSTERY GIFTS

TRUE LARGE PRINT

YES! Please send me 2 FREE Love Inspired® Suspense True Large Print novels and my 2 FREE mystery gifts (gifts are worth about $10). After receiving them, if I don't wish to receive any more books, I can return the shipping statement marked "cancel." If I don't cancel, I will receive 3 brand-new true large print novels every month and be billed just $7.99 per book in the U.S. or $9.99 per book in Canada. That's a savings of at least 20% off the cover price. It's quite a bargain! Shipping and handling is just 50¢ per book in the U.S. and 75¢ per book in Canada.* I understand that accepting the 2 free books and gifts places me under no obligation to buy anything. I can always return the shipment and cancel at any time. Even if I never buy another book, the two free books and gifts are mine to keep forever.

124/324 IDN F5GD

Name   (PLEASE PRINT)

Address   Apt. #

City   State/Prov.   Zip/Postal Code

Signature (if under 18, a parent or guardian must sign)

Mail to the **Harlequin® Reader Service:**
IN U.S.A.: P.O. Box 1867, Buffalo, NY 14240-1867
IN CANADA: P.O. Box 609, Fort Erie, Ontario L2A 5X3

* Terms and prices subject to change without notice. Prices do not include applicable taxes. Sales tax applicable in N.Y. Canadian residents will be charged applicable taxes. Offer not valid in Quebec. This offer is limited to one order per household. Not valid for current subscribers to Love Inspired Suspense True Large Print books. All orders subject to credit approval. Credit or debit balances in a customer's account(s) may be offset by any other outstanding balance owed by or to the customer. Please allow 4 to 6 weeks for delivery. Offer available while quantities last.

REQUEST YOUR FREE BOOKS!

2 FREE INSPIRATIONAL NOVELS IN TRUE LARGE PRINT

PLUS 2 FREE MYSTERY GIFTS

Love Inspired™

TRUE LARGE PRINT

YES! Please send me 2 FREE Love Inspired® True Large Print novels and my 2 FREE mystery gifts (gifts are worth about $10). After receiving them, if I don't wish to receive any more books, I can return the shipping statement marked "cancel." If I don't cancel, I will receive 3 brand-new true large print novels every month and be billed just $7.99 per book in the U.S. or $9.99 per book in Canada. That's a savings of at least 20% off the cover price. It's quite a bargain! Shipping and handling is just 50¢ per book in the U.S. and 75¢ per book in Canada.* I understand that accepting the 2 free books and gifts places me under no obligation to buy anything. I can always return the shipment and cancel at any time. Even if I never buy another book, the two free books and gifts are mine to keep forever.

117/317 IDN F5FZ

Name	(PLEASE PRINT)

Address	Apt. #

City	State/Prov.	Zip/Postal Code

Signature (if under 18, a parent or guardian must sign)

Mail to the **Harlequin® Reader Service:**
IN U.S.A.: P.O. Box 1867, Buffalo, NY 14240-1867
IN CANADA: P.O. Box 609, Fort Erie, Ontario L2A 5X3

* Terms and prices subject to change without notice. Prices do not include applicable taxes. Sales tax applicable in N.Y. Canadian residents will be charged applicable taxes. Offer not valid in Quebec. This offer is limited to one order per household. Not valid for current subscribers to Love Inspired True Large Print books. All orders subject to credit approval. Credit or debit balances in a customer's account(s) may be offset by any other outstanding balance owed by or to the customer. Please allow 4 to 6 weeks for delivery. Offer available while quantities last.

LITLP13TR

Reader Service.com

Manage your account online!

- Review your order history
- Manage your payments
- Update your address

---

*We've designed
the Harlequin® Reader Service
website just for you.*

Enjoy all the features!

- Reader excerpts from any series
- Respond to mailings and special monthly offers
- Discover new series available to you
- Browse the Bonus Bucks catalogue
- Share your feedback

Visit us at:

ReaderService.com

RS13TR